# Spark

····················································

## Allie Lasky

AES Publishing LLC

Cover Design by Jillian Liota, Blue Moon Creative Studio

Editing by Beth Hudson, Ink.

# Contents

-----------------------------------------

# Preface

-----------------------------------------

I've always wanted to write a book with characters like me.

Now that we have my gremlins, Chanukah has become my favorite holiday. I love seeing them experience the joy and exhilaration I remember so clearly from when I was a kid. To them, Chanukah isn't about presents, it truly is a Festival of Lights and love.

I went to a Jewish preschool, then Hebrew School from kindergarten through seventh grade, then Hebrew High through confirmation in tenth grade and graduation in twelfth grade. When I was thirteen, I had a Bat Mitzvah; I've read from the Torah, and I've recited the Haftorah at Yom Kippur services. Growing up, I was active in USY and Jewish summer camps, president of my temple's youth group in high school, and in college I even ran a temple's youth group chapter for five years. Every Rosh Hashanah and Yom Kippur, I spend the long days in temple with my family, and I've been to Passover Seders with over a hundred people (pre-Covid). Each month, I attend Tot Shabbat with my gremlins, and our family will have Shabbat dinner on Friday nights and bagel brunch on Sunday mornings.

Being Jewish is part of me, and I wouldn't be able to peel away the layers of my Jewish identity without taking away the things that make me who I am at my core.

For the queer, neurodivergent Jewish kids I knew so well growing up:
I truly am part of the tribe.

# Arielle

------------------------------------------------

## Thanksgiving weekend - Chicago suburbs

I can't breathe. There are too many people in here; they're packed in, tight, because Cole's is *the* place to be tonight. The music in the bar is loud, warring with the bubble of chatter from everyone talking and having a good time. In the corner, there are pool tables in use, the balls hitting the bumpers. Behind the bar, the staff pour drinks and swipe cards, and it's all—

It's too much.

Simon's hand lands on my elbow. "You good?" My big brother asks me. The thin band of his wedding ring feels heavy on my skin through the thick fabric of my sweater.

I swallow. Evaluate.

He's not trying to pity me. I know that. He's trying to make sure I genuinely am okay.

But the kindness in his eyes, and the furrow in his brow, makes me feel like I'm twelve years old again. I don't like it.

"I'm fine," I tell him.

"Arielle, it's okay to not be okay," he says quietly. I can hardly hear his voice in the hubbub of the bar, but I've already internalized the words.

Blowing out a breath, I rake my hand through my curls, untangling a snag almost on auto-pilot. "I'll be fine," I amend.

"You want a drink?" He jerks his head towards the bar.

"Sure. The usual."

My brother gives me a half-smile. "Be right back."

Shaina, my new sister-in-law, takes a seat beside me. "So… this is it?"

"It gets better," I assure her. Last year, they spent Thanksgiving with her family, and the year before, she and Simon were still spending holidays separately.

It's now the Friday night of Thanksgiving weekend. After two full days of "family time", I'm ready be back home… and my flight to Boston isn't until tomorrow midday. As much as I enjoy being in Chicago, I know I'll appreciate it even more once I'm in my own city, in my own apartment, in my own bed. My childhood bedroom doesn't feel like home anymore.

The crowd is a mix of faces I've seen before and new people I don't know. Cole's is the unofficial neighborhood hangout for my friends. It helps that Cole's younger brother, Caleb, was in my grade in school, and their cousin, Eric, was the year above Simon.

Because my brother and I are three years apart, our friend circles have always overlapped. Half of my friends from Hebrew School had siblings or cousins in the span between Simon and me, and even if they didn't—our community is so small, we all know each other in a roundabout way.

Molly Rubinstein walks past our table, then pauses and turns back. "Hey, Arielle."

I manage a smile for one of my oldest friends. "Hey. I didn't realize you were coming home!"

Our old Hebrew School group chat is... well, it's not dormant, but we don't utilize it very often. Mainly it's Asher, Estee, Hannah, and Ethan, arranging trips to one another's cities.

I don't travel for fun much. As it is, I'm on the road often enough for work, so when I have some time to myself, I like to spend it at home. Really, I could spend a week inside my apartment alone and only venture out for food, and I would be totally happy.

Other people? What do I need them for?

"Decided last minute," Molly says, and I blink. Oh, yeah. She came in from D.C. for the weekend. "My client struck a plea deal, so I hopped on a plane. It was... Well, it's nice to get away from everything."

"How do you like being a lawyer?" Last I heard, she was an underling in the District Attorney's office, getting her feet wet in her first year out of school.

She shrugs. "It's... Well, all I've ever done is school, so it's kind of different. But I like it."

My brother returns with three drinks. "Hey, Molls."

"Simon. Hey."

Shaina narrows her eyes.

"Have you met my wife?" My brother asks, a sappy grin on his face. "This is Shaina. We got married in September."

"Nice to meet you," Molly says. "I saw the wedding pictures online. You guys—wow, your dress was so gorgeous."

"Thanks," Shaina says, some of her coolness thawing.

Simon pushes a glass of moscato into my hand. "How's Robby?"

Molly's brother was in the year behind my brother. The four of us regularly got together.

"He's good. Still in Alaska." She shrugs. "He's doing his thing. He's happy. That's all I want for him."

"Well, tell him I say hi," Simon tells her.

"I will. I'm going to go get a drink," Molly declares. She jerks her head towards the front of the bar. "Some of us are hanging out. Do you want to join?"

"Go get your drink." I offer her a small smile. "I'll head out with you on your way back."

It's not that I don't want to hang out with my oldest friends. I do. I want to.

I want to *want* to.

But it's loud, and it's crowded, and it's hot, and it's just too much. Way too much.

And after a weekend of family, trodding on my reasonable boundaries...

Taking a sip of my moscato, I let the sweetness flood my senses. It's almost sickeningly sweet, which is just the way I like it, masking the taste of the alcohol.

"You don't have to," Simon tells me once Molly has moved on. "It's totally cool if you want to hang with us."

Shaina doesn't look so sure.

"No, it'll be good to see my friends," I say. "It'll be good for me."

I haven't been pushing myself. I've been letting myself go stagnant, and that's not good.

So when Molly approaches a few minutes later with a beer in her hands, I scoop up my coat and follow her.

There's a little alcove by the front window, and that's where my friends are gathered. It seems like my entire Hebrew School class is here tonight. Then again, that's not exactly difficult—there were only fifteen of us in our year, compared to twenty-three in the year ahead of us and thirty in the grade below us.

Estee Cohen lets out a shriek and barrels towards me. She wraps her arms around me, hugging tightly. She's been my best friend since we met when we were six, when my family moved to the neighborhood. We kept in touch through college, then while she was in law school on the west coast. But now she's back—well, we're both on the east coast, only a few hours train ride away rather than a whole country separating us.

"You two haven't changed." Noah Abramson grins, slinging his arm around Estee's shoulders in a side hug. He must remember I don't like to be hugged, because he offers me a high-five instead.

"How do you like New York?" I ask him.

He shrugs. "It's not Michigan." He went to U of M for both undergrad and law school, moving to the city last summer after graduation.

Sometimes it seems like my entire class went on to law school. Rationally, I know it's not true — but when there are six lawyers in a class of fifteen kids...

There are certain stereotypes for a reason, and yes, it's not uncommon for our community to be heavily involved in certain business sectors. My dad and Simon are doctors. Half my friends are lawyers. My cousins are in wealth management. Still more friends are pursuing postgrad degrees.

And then there's me. I'm on the marketing and social media team for Boston's baseball team. It's a great job, and I love it... but I'm very well aware I'm still early in my career, working my way up, and my title isn't nearly as impressive as some of my friends with their fancy MD or JD or PhD.

As I say hello to a group of people I've known for twenty years, a sense of contentment settles deep within me. The wine dulling my senses doesn't hurt, either. I'm still a little overstimulated, it's too loud and too crowded in here, and it's just *too much*, but somehow, being with everyone again soothes me in a way that I couldn't predict.

A shiver runs up my spine, and I turn to see Asher Gold cutting through the bar. He moves with confidence. The crowd parts and people turn to watch him pass. He's not the tallest guy, he's about a head taller than me, and he's a little thicker around the waist than he was last time I saw him. He's wearing a button-down shirt with the sleeves rolled up his strong forearms, dark jeans, and his Zeyde's watch.

He's always been gorgeous—that's never been in doubt. Now, with his curly hair styled short and his beard trimmed... Whew. The view is potent.

And when he joins our group, he sets his hand on my upper back, the warmth of his palm radiating through me.

"Hey, little Lion," he says softly, but I hear him perfectly. "How've you been?"

"Good," I choke out, then take a sip of my wine.

"Finally you join us," Estee teases him.

Asher shrugs. "Had things to do." He takes a pull on his beer, but he doesn't remove his hand from my back. "When did you get into town?" he asks me directly.

"Wednesday morning. I fly out tomorrow."

He frowns. "My flight's Sunday morning."

"Cool."

Sometimes I forget that we both live in Boston now. We don't hang out. I'm not entirely sure why. It just feels weird. He's part of my life here in Chicago. This is how I want to remember him. I don't know how it would work with him in my everyday life.

Caleb asks him a question, and the deep rumble of Asher's voice reverberates through me as they talk.

Okay. Look. I'm weak. I always have been when it comes to Asher Gold. He promised me a dance at my Bat Mitzvah, but I was nervous so I ran away from him. He was my first crush. Later, my first kiss.

But it never went beyond a chaste peck during a game of Spin the Bottle. I would die if he knew exactly how much that still had an effect on me more than ten years later.

He's always been easy with his affection—he's certainly never been stingy with me or the other girls in the class. Even with the guys, he's physically affectionate. But he's made it clear there are no romantic feelings involved in him holding hands with or hugging on someone.

Even if... My mood sours, and I take a drink of my wine.

Asher nods his head towards the corner, and I exhale as I follow him away from the crowd. We're pressed in against the window. Pulling up the sleeve of my oversized sweater, I press my hand against the sweaty glass.

It's cold, and it sends a tidal wave of relief through me.

"You doing okay?" His dark eyes are focused on my face.

"Why does everyone keep asking me that?"

Asher leans forward to speak, tucking a curl behind my ear. "Because I know you, and I know this is a lot. If it gets to be too much, let me know. I'm here for you."

My heart pounds. He doesn't mean it—not the way I wanted him to all those years ago. We're just friends. We've *always* just been friends. He just wants to make sure I don't have a public meltdown and embarrass him in front of half the neighborhood.

"Thanks," I whisper, then bring my wineglass to my lips. His eyes lock on mine as I take a sip.

I'm still overstimulated, but this time, it's fading into a buzzing hum in the back of my brain. Leaning against the cold plate glass of the window helps. The wine certainly helps. Asher smells good, like winter and apple pie spice, and—

Well, that doesn't exactly help.

"How was your holiday?" he asks.

"Fine."

He rolls his eyes. "So let me guess, your mother was a complete bitch, and your aunt said racist and homophobic things, and your cousins..."

I laugh, because he knows my family nearly as well as I do. "Yeah. Pretty much."

His parents live a few houses down from my aunt and uncle, so he's very familiar with their particular brand of hate. My actual cousins aren't bad, they're just so much younger than I am, it's hard to remember we have anything in common except genetics.

Asher sighs. "I'm so sorry."

"It is what it is," I say with a shrug. "How about you? Did your brother come home?"

He shakes his head. "Nope."

"Shit. That makes it..."

"Six years," he says. "We were twenty the last time he was here." He takes a sip of his beer. "He still talks to me, at least. He's okay. His wife is pregnant again. Their third."

"You're an uncle."

"I am," he acknowledges. "I see them maybe once a year, as schedules allow, but we video chat regularly. The kids know who I am."

Asher's always made it clear that his parents didn't disown Adam for marrying someone not Jewish. They would never do that, he likes to say, then roll his eyes to convey his sarcasm. For their parents, it was more the fact that Adam chose to marry someone from an entirely different culture, with an entirely different religion, and then they got pissed when Kashika refused to convert to a religion she didn't believe in "for the optics" of the wedding.

Last I heard, Adam didn't convert to Hinduism, either. They were married at the courthouse with her entire family in attendance, Asher by his side, then had a party in a downtown ballroom. I was away at college, but I saw the photos online.

It's funny. Adam and Kashika grew up two towns apart, but they had to go all the way to Tucson for college to meet.

"Are you dating anyone?" I ask Asher, and he chokes.

"Um, no. Not right now." He wipes the back of his hand over his mouth.

"Do you want to be?"

His eyes are dark. "Yeah. There's someone," he says.

Disappointment casts a dark cloud over me. "I hope it works out for you two," I tell him.

"Yeah, me too." He looks back over at our childhood friends. Nathan and Noah are on their phones, Ethan and Caleb are roughhousing, and Zippy, Dassy, and Estee are huddled together with Molly and Hannah.

I'm glad to be back with my friends. I've kept in touch with them through the years more than I have anyone else. There are a few girls from high school I keep up with, and the friends I made in college, but this group, these people... they're my home.

"Hey, you want to get out of here?" Asher asks.

Did I miss it, or are we standing closer together than we were before? He reaches out, twirling one of my loose curls around his finger, before he tucks it behind my ear again.

I look up at him. "And do what?"

He shrugs. "Go for a walk?"

"Yeah. That would be nice."

Asher opens his mouth, like he's about to say something, then shakes his head.

"What?" I ask.

"Nothing," he says.

I shove lightly at his bicep. "Come on, tell me."

"I'd rather show you," he says quietly.

"Okay...?"

He steps closer to me. His finger tilts my chin up. His warm breath fans over my face.

"Arielle," he whispers.

A bolt of lightning shoots through me.

Holy shit. Is he...

My phone rings, and he jolts away. I take a step back, but I'm against the window, so I can only go so far. I scramble for my phone in my back pocket.

My stomach sinks at the name and picture on the display.

Trevor.

*What am I doing?*

"I have a boyfriend," I tell Asher.

He goes white. "What?"

Swallowing, I shake my head. "I have to go. I'll see you around."

# Asher

-------------------------------------

**Two weeks later - Boston**


**Tuesday, Night 1**

I am a fucking idiot.

"Dude," Yoni says, kicking me under the table. "Cheer up."

I roll my eyes. It's easy for him to say. His life is pretty fucking perfect.

"Come on," he says. "It's not that bad."

It's the first night of Chanukah. This year, the holiday falls in the second week of December—a little early, but not abnormally so. We're at a bar in Allston, decorated in all non-denominational black and gold instead of red and green.

Okay, so it's not non-denominational so much as it's decorated for the local hockey team. It's a hockey bar. Then again, three quarters of the bars in the greater Boston area are hockey bars, especially at this time of year.

Yoni invited me to the Chanukah party his husband was organizing with his queer book club. I've gone to the book club twice in the four years I've lived in town, but I'm not interested in the sci-fi books they read, so Yoni and I use it as a time to grab a beer and hang out. Usually, we come here to watch a hockey game. It's just down the street from the lab where he works, and not far from the middle school where I teach seventh grade social studies.

"You didn't see it," I remind him.

"Look, you finally made a move, and she wasn't interested. It sucks, I get that, but it's not the end of the world."

Sighing, I pick at the label on my beer bottle. "Feels like it."

I'm still kicking myself for wrecking this fragile thing I had with Arielle. Connecting with her is always the highlight of my trips back home.

I don't know what I was thinking. There's no way she would have ever been interested in someone like me. When I saw her at Rosh Hashanah, it was right after her brother's wedding, and... well, I kind of thought she was giving me a hint when she mentioned settling down. But then she didn't talk to me in the nine weeks between the holidays and our friendly meetup over Thanksgiving, so...

So I went for it.

And then she gave me that bogus line about having a boyfriend. Except maybe it might not be so bogus—I did see a photo of her with a guy in Simon's wedding album. She certainly looked happy enough. Stupid of me to assume it was a cousin or a friend and not a *boyfriend*.

At least I don't have to see her until Passover next spring, if both of us even go back to Chicago for it. In the three years I've lived in Boston, we have met up twice for dinner and once to grab drinks, and all three occasions coincided with other friends being in town. The two of us don't spend time together. She's never been interested.

Fuck. I read that situation all wrong.

"Stop kicking yourself," Yoni tells me again. He nods towards the bar. "There's a group over there. They're hot. Go chat them up."

I glare at him. "You going to be my wingman?"

He laughs. "You're afraid of three pretty women?"

"I'm afraid of getting shot down in front of three pretty women."

But I do crane my neck to get a better look.

And then I freeze.

Because it's not just any group of women. Sure, two of them, I've probably never seen before. I don't care about them.

Arielle Weiss is here. She's in *my* local bar, having a drink, looking abso-fucking-lutely gorgeous, and...

"Why is she here?"

Yoni raises his eyebrows. "Who?"

I jerk my chin towards the group. "That's her."

His eyes bug out. "No shit. Seriously?"

Nodding, I let my eyes trail over her form. She's wearing dark jeans and an oversized dark green sweater, the sleeves rolled up to her elbows. Her curly brown hair is pinned back with little silver barrettes, which match the delicate silver chain around her neck.

She hasn't seen me. Good. I can slip out of here and—

"I need a beer," Yoni announces. He turns to Elliott. "You good, babe?"

His husband nods, in the middle of an intense conversation about world-building.

"C'mon, let's grab another round," Yoni says. "We can say hi, you can ask her to marry you, you know, the usual."

I glare at him again. "That is remarkably unsubtle."

My best friend laughs. "Fuck you, I'm not trying to be subtle."

With a sigh, I follow him across the room towards the bar. I barely notice the two other women sitting at the high-top table. My attention is laser-focused on her, the same way it always has been.

"She's hot," Yoni comments casually.

"Don't talk about her like that," I snap.

"I'm just saying. She's hot. You could do a lot worse."

I give his shoulder a sharp shove. "Lay off, okay? I'm just—I'm not in the mood."

"Okay, okay," he says, lifting his hands in surrender. "Can you at least introduce us?"

"Fuck you," I tell him, all good humor gone. I'm so *tired*.

Tired of being the butt of the joke.

Tired of being the only single guy in the group.

Tired of—*everything*.

I spin around, ready to grab my coat and leave, when his strong hand on my shoulder turns me back around.

"Ash, chill," Yoni says softly, his fingers curling around my shoulder. "I didn't mean anything by it. You're old friends. I want to meet her. I want to know everything."

Yoni and I are friends—best friends, but just friends. He's *married,* for fuck's sake. I was the one to hook him up with my ex, and he and Elliott work so much better together than El and I ever did.

I know he just wants the best for me. I know he just wants me to be even half as happy as he and El are.

"C'mon," I finally tell him. "I need a drink."

He grins, his smile lighting up his face. He claps me on the shoulder.

Together we make our way to the bar, and he places an order for the both of us, adding it to his tab.

He didn't have to buy my drink, but I like to think it's his way of apologizing.

Beer in hand, I take a deep breath and square my shoulders. Arielle is sitting with her friends, smiling, talking excitedly. Her hands fly as she talks, illustrating her point, and with one quick movement she nearly upends her wineglass.

With practiced movement, she steadies her glass before she continues with her story. She hasn't noticed me—good. I can pause, reassess, evaluate.

How do I want to do this?

How do I talk to the woman I've been pining over for months, when the last time I saw her, she brutally rejected me?

"You've got this," Yoni murmurs.

And then he shoves me forward.

Fucker.

I nearly trip over my feet, catching myself at the last moment. It's not enough time to stop me from crashing into Arielle's chair from behind, though.

She squeals and whips around, her eyes blazing. "Ex-*cuse*—"

Her eyes bug out.

"Asher?" Her voice is high-pitched and squeaky. "What are you doing here?"

"Hanging out with some friends," I say, nodding towards our table. Elliott is watching us, a faint smile on their face. "Saw you, wanted to come over and say hi."

She bites her lip. "Hi?"

There are two other women at the table, both dark-haired with olive skin and dark eyes. The one on the left is wearing a *chai* necklace. They look—they're average. I'm sure another guy, someone who's more interested, might find them pretty. Perfectly adequate. It's just that there's nobody in this world that could possibly compare to Arielle Weiss in any respect. She's got brains and beauty, all wrapped up in a genuine kindness that outshines everyone else.

Yoni clears his throat.

"Arielle and I grew up together," I say, looking over at her friends, who are watching with amusement on their faces. "We were—friends."

She scowls, and I wonder what I did to cause that reaction.

Just because she has a boyfriend doesn't mean she and I can't be friends. I've known her since we were six years old.

She's my friend, even if I only see her a few times a year and we only talk when we're both home.

Just because I want it to be more than that doesn't mean we can't enjoy our shared history.

She's my friend.

"Oh, and this is Yoni," I add lamely.

He elbows me. "He hasn't stopped talking about you," he tells Arielle, which makes her flush and look away.

"And you're *here*?" She looks around the bar.

"My friend's book club is having their Chanukah party."

Arielle frowns.

Unease prickles at the back of my neck. She doesn't look happy to see me. Would she prefer I just ignored her and pretended I didn't recognize her from across the bar?

"How's the boyfriend?" I ask with forced lightness to my tone.

Arielle picks up her half-full wineglass and takes a hearty gulp, draining it in two swallows.

"Oh, look, my glass is empty," she says sarcastically. "I'll be right back."

"Oh... okay," I say.

She pushes back her chair.

But she doesn't head to the bar.

No—to my surprise, she picks up her coat and her purse, and walks out of the bar.

"Fuck," I exhale, pinching the bridge of my nose.

"Yeah, that didn't go well at all," the friend on the right says.

Uncomfortable, I glance over at her. She's smiling politely.

"What's the chance she's coming back?" Yoni asks.

The two women look at each other. They burst out laughing.

"Great." I sigh.

"I'm Rachel," says the friend on the left. "This is Sadie."

"Nice to meet you," my best friend offers.

"So you're the Thanksgiving break guy," Sadie says slowly.

Yoni nods enthusiastically, clapping me on the shoulder. "He just wanted to clear the air."

"Does *he* know how to talk?" Rachel asks with a snide tone.

I'm too emotionally wrung out to bristle.

"I just want to talk to her," I say quietly.

Rachel sighs, relaxing some of the tension in her shoulders. "I'm sure another time, she'd be in a great place to talk. Tonight, though..."

My heart pounds. "Did she have a bad day?"

Sadie purses her lips. "It..."

"She looked like she was happy. Cheerful," I add. "And then we came over, and she..." I sigh again. "I just want to talk to her."

Rachel and Sadie have a silent conversation. After a moment, Rachel turns to me.

"Give me your phone," she says.

"Excuse me?" My voice cracks.

"I'm going to give you my number," she says.

"Look, I—you're great, you're gorgeous, but—"

Rachel bursts out laughing. "Dude, no. I'm not hitting on you."

I blow out a breath. "Okay. Good. Because—"

"Because you totally have the hots for Arielle. Look, I get it," she says. She waves her hand in front of me. "Phone, dude."

Suppressing a laugh, I hand it over.

"We're going to the theatre tomorrow night," Sadie adds in. "And I'm feeling—*ahem*—sick." She coughs theatrically.

"My boss is going to need me to stay late at the office and finish an emergency project," Rachel says. She types in her number, then a moment later, her phone vibrates in front of her. "I'll text you my ticket. I won't tell her I'm cancelling until right before curtain, so she won't have a chance to bail."

With a frown, I say, "Isn't that dishonest? I mean, she's going to be upset that you guys won't be there."

Yoni smacks my shoulder. "Dude, they're setting you up."

I blink.

"She's guaranteed to be there, she thinks she's meeting with them, and instead you'll be there," he continues. "You'll watch the show, maybe put your arm around her shoulders and snuggle."

"Or she'll slap me across the face and walk out," I counter.

He sucks his teeth. "Yeah, or maybe that."

Sadie grins at me. "Only one way to find out."

# Arielle

----------------------------------------

## Wednesday, Night 2

**M**y hands shake. My friends and I had plans to see a touring Broadway musical tonight, and they bailed. Sadie is under the weather, and Rachel is slammed at work, and—

I don't want to cancel. I don't want to miss the show.

But I also don't want to do this by myself.

I have no issue going to the movies by myself.

Eating in a restaurant? Totally cool.

Traveling? In fact, I prefer to travel alone.

But the theatre? That's an experience meant to be *shared*.

Oh, well. It's too late to back out, and I'm already in the lobby. I'm *here*. I can't back out now. I've been dying to see this show for the last two years, and I'm so glad it came to town.

After a quick perusal of the merch stand—nothing I want or need, this time—and a stop at the bar for a hot cocoa, I make my way to my seats in the back of the lower level.

We lucked out into these seats. They were actually cheaper in the second to last row of the orchestra, than in the first row of the upper-most balcony. And when you split the cost of season tickets across six shows that I'd want to see no matter what, it actually ends up being quite affordable.

Plus, there are all sorts of season ticket member perks, like a discount on drinks, sales on other shows not part of the package, and first access to new events and programs.

Also, it makes me feel really grown up to have season tickets to the theater. I'm only twenty-six, and sometimes that makes me feel old and withered, but most of the time I feel like I'm faking this whole adult thing. Four years ago when I graduated from college, I moved to the city, I found a stable job, and I got an apartment with great roommates, but I still have to Google how to do basic life skills like sew a button back onto my coat and the proper way to deep clean a bathroom.

I'm not in a hurry to *grow up*, per se. I'm just wondering when it will hit me that I'm a mostly financially stable adult-type person who can live off their income and somehow save money *and* have extra left over for fun, frivolous things like theater tickets.

I've avoided it long enough; I need to go to my seat, my friends' left empty, and force my brain to quiet down so I can enjoy the show.

But there's someone in my row. There's someone sitting in our section.

Asher Gold is sitting in Rachel's seat, the middle of our trio.

That bitch. She set me up. No way is she working late.

And I'm guessing Sadie isn't sick at all. She was just fine last night.

Heat rises uncomfortably to my face. They played me. They tricked me.

It feels like eighth grade all over again, when the popular girls in school would play pranks on me, and I couldn't understand the joke.

My friends stood up for me. Asher, Estee, Hannah, Ethan... they made those tough years bearable.

I know Sadie and Rachel want the best for me... but sometimes we might disagree on what the best option might actually be.

Asher's head swivels in my direction, and his eyes go wide. He swallows.

He looks good. He's wearing slacks and a light blue dress shirt, a dark green tie around his neck. His short, curly hair is styled neatly, and—did he trim his beard?

And then he's standing, pressing the backs of his legs into the back of the seat, and I catch a whiff of the ginger and clove of his cologne as I scoot past him to my assigned seat.

"I suppose I should ask what you're doing here," I say bitterly to the red velvet curtain on the stage at the front of the theater, "but I'm guessing I won't get a straight answer out of you."

"I just want to talk to you," he says. He turns to look at me.

There's a lump in my throat. I can't look at him. I don't *want* to look at him.

I've never been very good at ignoring him, though.

"I want to apologize," he blurts.

My heart stops. "What?" I shift in my seat and face him.

He's gazing at me with sorrow in his eyes. He looks genuinely contrite.

"That night at Cole's... I overstepped," Asher says. "I behaved inappropriately. I'm sorry for the way I acted. And I'm sorry to have scared you or made you uncomfortable. That's the last thing I want, little lion."

The sound of my old nickname makes me take a sharp breath. It's something my friends used to call me after we learned the origins of our names in fourth grade. For three years, everyone bought me lion everything—plushies, t-shirts, photos. Anything I could possibly be gifted all had a lion theme.

In Hebrew, my name means Lion of G-d.

In *The Lion King*, Nala is the lioness best friend who grows up alongside Simba. She is the strong, capable, fierce protector who brings the King back home and restores balance to Pride Rock.

I am strong.

I am capable.

I am fierce.

I am a lion.

"I don't ever want to jeopardize our friendship," he continues. "We've known each other for twenty years. You're one of my oldest friends. And we're here, living in the same city. I don't—I want us to be friends."

My stomach sinks. "Friends?"

He nods. "We're both here, so far from home... it would be nice to be able to hang out and have a little normalcy sometimes." He shrugs. "No pressure. I don't expect us to suddenly be attached at the hip. I liked your friends last night. I want to meet the boyfriend. I want to *know* you, in whatever way you'll let me, both here and in Chicago."

"Asher..." I need to tell him—about Trevor, about everything, all the thoughts running through my head the last few weeks.

"Just think about it," he says quietly. "I'm not pushing. If you're really not interested, that's okay. We don't have to hang out. I just thought..."

"Yes," I blurt.

He blinks.

"I want that," I tell him.

"Great," he says, but his eyes are dark. "We're friends again."

I open the program in my hands. Shifting in my seat, I try to get comfortable. Asher's shoulders are broad, and while he's not exactly *manspreading*, his knees aren't exactly squeezed together, either. The outside of his knee brushes against the fabric of my skirt. I can feel the heat radiating off his body like a furnace, warming me inside and out.

"I didn't take you as a theater fan," I comment lightly.

"There's a lot you don't know about me," he says with an equally light tone. "It's been a long time since we've hung out. A conversation at temple or at the bar isn't exactly enough for much more than catching up."

"So... tell me. You're a teacher," I say, counting on my fingers. "You live in—are you still in Dorchester?"

"I'm in Malden now, actually."

"Oh. I'm in Medford."

That's the neighborhood right next door. What a small world.

"You keep up with your brother, you like your job..." I bite my lip. "Have you dated anyone recently?"

He squints at me. "In the two weeks since Thanksgiving?"

"In the four years since we graduated from college and you broke up with what's-her-face, the girl who got upset whenever we messaged in the group chat."

"Shira? I haven't talked to her in years." He shudders, then laughs. "I had a boyfriend for a while. It didn't work out." He shrugs. "We're still friends, introduced them to their husband. Was best man at the wedding."

Oh. That's right.

He's bisexual.

Sometimes it's easy to forget. Most of the relationships I've seen him post about on social media were with women. Aside from a guy he met at summer camp when we were fifteen or sixteen, and then a guy he met through his fraternity in college, I don't remember him talking about guys very much.

But that's on me for assuming. His bisexuality doesn't get erased just because he dates women more often than he dates men, either publicly or privately. At his core, he's still the same person no matter the gender identity of his partner. At his core, his own sexual orientation doesn't change based on who he may or may not be dating.

I remember when my brother's friend Oren came out in my sophomore year during a game of Truth or Dare, the guy was so scared he was shaking... and then Asher just calmly announced that he was bisexual, and if anyone had a problem with either of them, he'd take care of it.

Nobody had a problem with it, of course. Once the initial shock wore off—about two minutes—we were all back to usual.

In fact, it was later at that same party that Asher kissed me—during a game of Spin the Bottle, of course, because there was no way he'd ever actually be interested in me as a potential partner.

"Do you—"

I cut off abruptly as the lights start to dim.

Asher reaches over and squeezes my knee. "We'll chat later," he promises.

I'm sad when he pulls away and straightens in his seat. Shifting, I angle ever so slightly closer, enough to get another whiff of his warm, familiar scent.

In the darkening theatre, he shoots me a half-smile, and my stomach flips with butterflies and caterpillars.

How are we supposed to do this? How do we navigate this? I want to keep our flagging friendship alive, but I don't know how that works now that we're all grown up. Can we even still be friends?

# Asher

----------------------------------------

## Thursday, Night 3

The holiday craft fair is not exactly my idea of a fun time. But when Arielle texted asking if I wanted to go, I couldn't say no. There's never been much I've been able to deny her.

Her friends Sadie and Rachel are here with her, too. No boyfriend, though.

Was it all just a convenient lie? Did she make him up to politely turn me down?

My eyes drink in the sight of her. Arielle is wearing her dark, curly hair loose around her shoulders, topped by a royal blue knit beanie with a little pom-pom on the crown. She's fully covered by a thick winter coat, a scarf that looks handmade, knee-high snow boots, and dark leggings. Even her hands are covered in royal blue mittens that match her beanie and scarf. The only skin visible is her face, and she—

She looks gorgeous.

Not that she doesn't usually. She does. She's downright beautiful.

But when she turns and catches sight of me, and her dark eyes widen, then shine brightly like glittering topaz stones...

"Hey, little lion," I say as I approach. To my surprise, when I open my arms for a hug, she folds into them readily. The top of her head reaches my chin, so the pom-pom on her hat tickles my nose. I breathe in the stark, wintery scent of her, citrus and bright, with a sharp bite of snow on the horizon.

Am I imagining it, or does she not want to let me go?

A throat clears behind me. I've brought Yoni and Elliott with me for backup. I'm not sure that I *need* them here, but—I'd like to have some moral support, plus maybe if we couch this whole thing as *friends* being *friends* in the company of other *friends*... I might get it through my thick skull that she isn't actually interested in me.

Even if the rejection still stings, two and a half weeks later.

With a sigh, I release her and take a step back. Her cheeks are rosy red from the cold. Already, I miss the feeling of her in my arms.

"You guys remember Yoni," I introduce. Sadie nods, and Rachel checks him out. "This is his husband."

"I'm Elliott, and my pronouns are they/them," they say.

"Nice to meet you," Arielle says.

"So, craft fair," Yoni says lightly.

"Some of my favorite memories are the craft fairs the elementary school used to host," Arielle answers. "They'd put up folding tables on the stage in the auditorium, and—"

"I remember those," I chime in. "You always liked the homemade marshmallows."

Her cheeks get pink. "You remember that?"

With a nod, I clear my throat and shove my hands in my coat pockets. I remember a lot where Arielle Weiss is concerned.

"I know we're already a third of the way through Chanukah, but it's not about the gifts. It's about the present," she says firmly. "And I like to support the local artists. They deserve to have their art displayed, and if I happen to find a gift for someone at the same time, well, it doesn't have to be a holiday gift, it can be just because."

"I like that philosophy," Elliott says, and she beams at them. They release Yoni's hand and step to her, linking their arm through hers. "So, tell me. How long have you and Asher known each other?"

Oh.

Oh shit.

It just hit me that I've introduced Arielle to my ex. The ex who knows *a little too much* about me.

But if she recognizes that Elliott and I have history, Arielle doesn't comment.

"We grew up together," she says, giving me a fond smile. "It's been, what, twenty years?"

"You moved to the neighborhood when you were six, right before first grade," I say.

Rachel and Sadie glance at each other, then break into grins. I swear Rachel winks at me.

"So yeah, we've known each other for a long time," I finish lamely.

"And how is this the first time we've all hung out in a group?" Elliott continues. "How long have you lived in Boston?"

"About four years. Ash and I mostly hang out when friends come into town," Arielle says. "I'm way too boring the rest of the time."

There's an elephant sitting on my chest. Is that what she thinks?

Is that how she thinks *I* view her?

Because that can't be farther from the truth.

Opening my mouth, I want to interject, but Yoni shoves me roughly.

"Let's go in," he says. "I want to find a present for my niece's birthday."

How did we end up like this? I wanted to spend time with Arielle, not hook her up with my ex.

To my surprise, Sadie moves towards me, then wraps her arm around my elbow.

"We didn't get a chance to talk much the other night," she comments as she steers me toward the entrance to the fair. "Rach kind of ran the show."

I force a laugh. "Yeah, I guess so."

"You have our support, in case that wasn't clear," she adds. "Both of us."

Glancing down at her, she's smiling, her eyes on Arielle and Elliott a few paces ahead. They've stopped at the first table, admiring the snowflake earrings a vendor has displayed.

Yoni and Rach are behind us, talking quietly. I don't know what they're talking about, and I feel guilty for dumping my friend with a virtual stranger, but he doesn't seem to mind.

"Thanks. That means a lot."

"She needs someone like you in her life."

"What about the boyfriend?" My question comes out more frustrated than I intended.

Sadie's eyes go wide. "She hasn't talked to you about him?"

I shake my head.

"Dude, you guys need to sit down and have a conversation," she says. "Just—clear the air."

"I'd love to, except every time I try to talk to her, she changes the subject."

Or she runs away like at the bar, or the curtain rises like at the theatre last night.

"Just keep trying," Sadie suggests, squeezing my arm. "It'll be worth it."

"*She* is worth it," I agree.

Her friend smiles up at me. "I knew it."

"Knew what?"

"That you see her."

I sigh. "All I can see is her."

Sadie shakes her head. "No. You *see* her. You know her. Quirks and all."

"Being neurodivergent isn't a quirk," I tell her.

"No, but you accept her because of it, rather than in spite of it." She frowns. "It's hard for her. Not everyone does. And I know it weighs on her."

"We've been friends since we were kids," I remind her. "Sure, we might not be all that close right now, but I know her. I know who she is. I like her just the way she is."

I stop in my tracks.

It's the first time I've said out loud that I like Arielle.

I mean, I wasn't running from the sentiment. For fuck's sake, I tried to kiss her. I've been trying to get close to her all week, since I saw her at the bar.

Sadie beams at me. "It'll work out," she assures me.

With a scowl, I start walking again, and she falls into step beside me, her arm still wrapped around my elbow. "But the boyfriend..."

"Don't worry about Trevor," she says. "He's an inconsequential blip in the span of her lifetime. You're not."

"How do you know that?"

"Because it's been twenty years, and you're still here, trying."

"I'd try for twenty more," I mutter.

She laughs. "See? That's how I know."

"I hope you're right."

"Don't worry," Sadie assures me. "I always am."

# Arielle

------------------------------------

I absolutely adore Elliott. It would be difficult not to. They're just so...

"C'mon," they urge me. "Why haven't you?"

In about fifteen seconds, they managed to coax out the admission that I have feelings for Asher. It's not like I was all that subtle. I know he's always been big on physical touch, that's his love language, but seeing him wrap himself around Sadie makes me itchy and hot. And not in a good way.

"It's complicated," I finally say.

Elliott rolls their eyes. "Yeah, okay. Whatever. Me and Asher are complicated. You two are—"

I pause. "You and Asher?"

Their eyes widen. "Oh. You didn't know?"

In response, my eyes narrow. "Know what?"

"Asher and I were together for a while." Elliott shrugs. "It didn't work out, it's fine, we're better as friends. He introduced me to Yoni, then he was the best man at our wedding. Yoni and I wouldn't be together if not for him."

They shoot a fond smile at their husband, who's accompanying Rachel through the craft fair.

"I didn't realize you two were together. You and Asher, I mean. I knew about Yoni. He's—I'm going to stop talking now," I announce.

"We dated. It didn't work out," they say simply. Their eyes narrow. "You knew he was bi. Is that what's holding you back?"

"I was there when he came out to our friends," I answer firmly. "He's dated guys before, he's dated women. It's part of who he is. That would never bother me."

"So then what's the issue?"

I look away and cross my arms over my chest, hiding away from my embarrassment.

"Tell me," they say softly. "Arielle..."

"You've seen him naked," I whisper, pained.

Their eyes flick to mine, surprised. "You care that he's a little thick?"

It's my turn to be surprised. "What? No! Are you kidding? He's so hot."

"Then what?"

"I've never been friends with someone who's also been with my partner," I say quietly. "I don't like the thought of you and Asher together."

They wait.

"I don't care about your gender or your orientation or pronouns. It's not that," I assure them. "It's the fact that you know him and you've had experiences with him that I can't even begin to comprehend. And I'll always worry about how I measure up to you, or to any of the others."

To my surprise, Elliott grins. "I like you, little lion," they announce in return. "And I'm pretty damn sure he likes you, too."

Sullenly, I scuff the toe of my boot into the sidewalk. "I don't know about that."

"Trust me, then."

"I hardly know you."

Elliott just takes my hand and leads me over to the next craft booth. "You know enough."

I roll my eyes.

"You know I love Asher," they say quietly. When I glance at them out of the corner of my eye, they shrug. "I'm not *in love* with him. I love him. He's family."

A hundred feet ahead of us, I hear his deep, throaty laugh. White hot ire rushes through me. Why is he laughing? Why is *Sadie* the one making him laugh? I want to be the one. I want to—

"I just want what's best for him," Elliott continues. They squeeze my mittened hand. "And I think you do, too."

"I do," I admit quietly.

They offer me a gentle smile. "Then I think we're all in agreement."

"What are we agreeing?" Rachel asks, behind us. I turn, and she's standing right there. Yoni has a cup of hot cocoa in his hand, a gift bag in the other.

"Ash is totally in love with her," Elliott announces. "And the feeling is very obviously mutual."

My face flames. I look away, my cheeks on fire.

"So we're going to figure out a way to get them together," they continue. "Who's in?"

Rachel shoves her arm into the air. "Me, me! Pick me!"

"I guess I could be persuaded..." Yoni trails off, then winks at me. "You should have seen him when he saw you at the bar. All he wanted to do was talk to you."

I bite my lip. "I don't know..."

"Forget about Trevor," Rachel tells me. "He's inconsequential."

My eyes narrow. "Excuse me?"

"In the grand scheme of your life, you'll forget about him. He's a non-issue," she says firmly. "Do you like Asher?"

I glare at her, frustrated at being called out so directly. "Yes. You know I do."

"Do you want what's best for him?" she continues.

Nodding, I hunch my shoulders, folding in on myself. "I do."

"Then why the fuck aren't you making a move?" Yoni demands.

"He doesn't feel the same way," I insist.

Elliott rolls their eyes.

"He doesn't. There's no way."

"I've known him for a long time," Yoni says. "Not as long as you guys, obviously. But I know when he has feelings for someone, and I know when he's kicking himself for messing things up."

"He didn't mess anything up." I squint at him. "What are you talking about?"

He shrugs. "I'm just saying, he thinks he did."

With a sigh, I scrub my hand over my face. "Okay. Fine. Whatever."

Elliott laughs.

"What do I do? How do I fix this?"

Yoni smirks. "I've got some ideas..."

***

## Saturday, Night 5

I can't believe I'm doing this. I've never crashed a wedding before. It's so *rude*.

Yoni and Elliott assured me that the bride and groom wouldn't care. In fact, I got a text from the maid of honor, Kate, encouraging me to show up.

It's a little weird to know that *all* of Asher's friends now know about my feelings for him. Especially when I haven't had a chance to tell him directly.

I don't know that I'll ever be able to do that, honestly.

Yoni and Asher are both in the wedding party, so I spend time with Elliott in the pre-wedding cocktail hour. They're wearing a deep green suit, and it looks absolutely amazing.

"Hey, little Lion," they say, offering me a tight hug. "Let me introduce you to some people."

I take a quick breath. "Okay."

"No more exes, at least not that I'm aware." They wink at me. "I wouldn't do that to you."

"Thanks," I whisper.

And when they take my hand, I let them pull me into the party.

There are more than a few eyes on us. People clearly know Elliott—everyone stops them to say hello—and they're all even more curious about the woman on their arm.

I don't know why. I'm nothing to get excited about. I'm just... me.

"He's been single for a while," Elliott comments idly.

"Excuse me?"

"He was seeing someone at the start of the year, but they broke up at Passover. Right after he went home and saw you," they say.

My eyes flash to theirs. "What?"

They shrug. "He didn't take her home for the Seder. I don't know the details. They weren't together very long. I just know he broke it off with her right around that time."

My stomach swirls. I barely even remember seeing him last April. We ran into each other at the grocery store—I was picking up some extra matzah, and he'd been sent out for milk and eggs. We talked for a few minutes in the dairy aisle. Maybe five, ten minutes? It was a blip of a conversation. I hardly remember it. Asher and I have known each other for so long...

"I..."

Elliott squeezes my arm. "I just don't think this is as one-sided as you seem to think it is."

My mind reels. I feel physically nauseous. "I had no idea. I hate the thought that he broke up with her for..."

"He thought it was worth it," they remind me quietly.

I bite my lip.

"Oh, come here," Elliott says, wrapping me in their arms. My head fits perfectly on their shoulder, and they squeeze me with steady pressure.

I'm not usually a fan of physical contact, especially with people I don't know well. I especially don't like hugs.

"Asher told me you like this," they say. "Firm, unrelenting pressure."

I sniffle. "I like it with him."

They freeze. "Should I not...?"

I cling to them. "Keep hugging," I whisper.

Inside my head, my thoughts race too fast for me to process. Asher knows what kind of hugs I like? I don't think I've ever mentioned it. Maybe once or twice over the last few years. I've gone over why I don't like hugs—that hasn't changed since I was a kid—but the last time I explained why was… back in high school? Maybe even in middle school. After I told all my friends, they just accepted it, and didn't question me.

We've done perfunctory hugs. I only let a few people hug me. My parents, my brother Simon, Estee, sometimes Rach and Sadie… and Asher.

And, now, Elliott.

"Come on," they tell me, with a finger on my chin. "Let's go sit down, and we can regroup until we're ready to see him again."

I nod against their shoulder. "That sounds good."

"Do you know what you're going to say?"

"… no," I admit.

"Don't worry, we'll figure it out. We'll come up with a good, heartfelt speech," they tell me with a smile. "It'll be worth it. I promise."

# Asher

--------------------------------------------

## Saturday, Night 5

Alex's wedding is fine. I'm wearing the tux, I'm paired up with a bridesmaid, his cousin Elise, and I walk her down the aisle before taking my place at the front of the room at the front of the room where the wedding *chuppah* is constructed.

In front of me, Yoni looks out into the crowd, and he smiles when he catches sight of his husband. I glance in Elliott's direction, and—

And then I freeze.

Because there is Arielle, wearing a fitted silver and navy dress, her curly hair cascading in a fancy waterfall over one shoulder.

It's like I've been punched in the gut. What's she doing here? What's she doing with *Elliott*? When I introduced them the other night, I never thought they'd get along so well that she wouldn't have time for me all night long...

Every time I turned around, they were together, whispering and giggling. Elliott had their arm around her, or she was holding their hand, or they were otherwise touching.

Arielle doesn't like to be touched. I know that, everyone knows that. After the craft fair, I pulled Elliott aside and warned them.

But here she is, curling into their side, their arm draped around her shoulder.

I want that. I want to be the one sitting beside her, holding her.

She's glancing behind her, taking in the bride and her parents—in Jewish weddings, it is not customary to rise when the bride comes into the room—and I know the moment she realizes I've spotted her.

Arielle's back goes ramrod straight. She clenches her jaw, and as she slowly turns around to face the *chuppah*, she meets my eyes and raises her chin in defiance.

I break into a giant smile. She's here. She's *here*. She isn't friends with Alex and Mara, she said the other day she'd never met them, but for her to be here...

Hope blooms deep within me. Maybe I haven't been imagining this. Maybe, possibly, she might one day return feelings for me...

But the boyfriend.

Was that a lie to avoid kissing me?

Does he even exist?

Both she and her friends referenced the same guy, some dude named Trevor.

I want to know who he is. I'm not a violent person, but I want to bash his face in. Just for existing.

Tentatively, Arielle smiles at me, and I beam back at her.

She's *here*.

We can recreate the opportunity we lost at her bat mitzvah. I'd asked her to dance at the next slow song, and she'd said yes, and then the DJ cut in with *Cha Cha Slide*, and by the time the next slow song came on, she was nowhere to be found.

I hadn't thought about that night for the last thirteen years, but when I saw her at the bar on Thanksgiving, it rushed back into my memory.

We only see each other a few times a year, mostly back home in Chicago. At Passover, we ran into each other at the grocery store. At Rosh Hashanah, we chatted in the temple lobby during the Yizkor service—there was a group of us, but she talked to *me* the most.

That's when I started thinking of her differently. She's always been there, in the periphery of my mind. But that was when I realized I wanted her to be front and center.

I like her. I think I've liked her for a while. But now I *see* her, and I like what I see.

Not just physically. Yes, she's beautiful. Very physically attractive.

But all the rest... she's smart, and she's kind, and she has the quickest wit I've ever known. For someone who doesn't always understand sarcasm, she sure wields it expertly. And she's funny, gut-clutching hilarious when she wants to be.

I like Arielle Weiss.

I like Arielle Weiss, and I'm going to tell her.

As the couple say their vows, I keep my eyes on Arielle. I wonder if she's ever thought about getting married—in general, not to me. Of course not to me. Her brother was just married a few months ago. I saw the wedding photos online. She looked gorgeous, outshining the bride in every picture. It was almost unfair.

And to my surprise, Arielle is looking back at me. She smiles softly, and as the rabbi recites the seven blessings to seal the ceremony, I swear Arielle wipes a tear from her eye.

I want this. I want this with her.

I want to love and cherish her. I want to honor her. I want to appreciate her, and show her how much I do, every single day. I want her to be mine—

But more than that, I want to be *hers*.

I want to be the person she calls when she needs to talk out her thoughts. I want to be the one she rants and vents to. I want to help her, support her, in any way she needs. Emotionally, mentally, physically, spiritually...

I want to love her.

Ahead of me, Yoni clears his throat, and I force my attention back to the couple as Alex lifts his foot and stomps on the glass.

"Mazal tov," the crowd cheers, as Alex and Mara kiss for the first time as a married couple.

Everyone is looking at them. Everyone is watching them.

And I'm looking at Arielle, who is watching me.

When I wink at her, she blushes and ducks her head, but then she raises her eyes back to mine.

Yeah. This is it. I'm done. I'm gone.

I am one hundred and fifteen percent totally and completely head over heels for Arielle Weiss.

After Alex and Mara traipse up the aisle for their *yichud*, their private time together to reflect upon their marriage, I escort my assigned bridesmaid up the aisle after them, then immediately head off the direction of the seating chart. I'm at a table with Yoni and Elliott, I know, but...

When I see the table assignments, I let out a relieved sigh. She's there. Her name is on the place setting directly beside mine.

Since I haven't been in a relationship in a while, Alex didn't offer me a plus-one to the wedding, but he's made it clear over the last few months since I broke it off with my last girlfriend that it would change if I found someone I was serious about. More than a passing fancy, he'd said, and then laughed.

I didn't laugh.

It's true that I've dated around. When I found someone that was a good match, I wasn't afraid of a serious relationship, but after Elliott and I broke up, it was with the knowledge that I wanted something as real as what they found with Yoni.

I found someone. I found *her*.

And now she's here, and she's at my friend's wedding, and she's...

There's a tap on my shoulder, and I turn to see Arielle standing there, blinking up at me. My heart nearly bursts out of my chest to attach itself to hers.

"Hi," she whispers.

"Hi," I whisper back.

She swallows. "I, um..."

"What are you doing here?"

Arielle's face falls. "Oh. Should I go?"

Confused, I blink back at her. "No? What? No. Don't leave. Never leave."

Shit. Did that sound too needy? I don't want to scare her off.

Just because I've come to this realization doesn't mean she's ready for what I want.

She might only want a casual fuck.

She might want to be friends.

She might not want forever.

I clear my throat. "I mean..."

Arielle bites her lip.

"I'm really glad you're here," I admit.

A shy smile spreads over her face. "You are?"

Nodding, I reach out and take her hand.

And when she doesn't pull away, when she looks up at me with that smile...

I start to hope.

Maybe this can be real.

Maybe this can be more than a one-time thing.

Maybe this is the real thing.

I want it to be.

"We should find our table," I tell her.

Arielle swallows again. "Okay. Sure."

"I do believe you owe me a dance," I tease.

She frowns up at me, her brow furrowed. "I do?"

With a nod, I smooth away the wrinkle in her forehead, and she smiles softly.

"From your Bat Mitzvah. You promised me a dance. I'm cashing it in."

She presses her lips together, ducking her head and looking away. "If you want..."

"I do," I tell her, stepping closer. "I haven't forgotten. I've just been waiting."

Arielle takes a deep breath.

"Me, too," she admits.

My heart pounds. She has? She didn't forget?

"It's been thirteen years," I say lightly, like I didn't know our Bar and Bat Mitzvahs were exactly half our lifetime ago.

She shrugs. "I can be patient."

I squeeze her hand. "You don't have to wait any more."

# Arielle

------------------------------------------------

Asher's hand in mine is a soothing balm to all my ruffled worries. Now that I'm here, now that I'm face to face with him... I'm starting to lose my nerve.

How do we do this?

Our table is at the front of the ballroom, adjacent to the head table. Asher and I are seated with Yoni and Elliott, as well as another groomsman, two bridesmaids, and their accompanying dates.

The other groomsman looks at me, then Asher's hand on mine, before he turns to the bridesmaids.

"Pay up," he says with a sly smirk.

The two women roll their eyes.

"What's this?" Asher asks.

"You've been agitated all day," one of the bridesmaids says. "Now we know why." She nods at me. "Hi. I'm Elise. Nice to meet you."

"Hi," I say quietly, waving awkwardly with my free hand. "I'm—"

"You're Arielle, right?" Asks the other bridesmaid. "I'm Kate. We've heard all about you."

I turn to Asher, who's blushing. "What have you said?"

He shrugs, not looking at me. "You know…"

"No, I don't." I try to disentangle our fingers. "Is this like that time at summer camp where—"

His face goes slack. "No. Not at all," he assures me quickly.

It's clear he remembers the mean girls in my cabin who thought I was weird and off-putting, and made no secret of their disdain for me.

"I just… I mentioned the other night, the craft fair," he says.

"And? To what purpose?"

He shakes his head. "We'll talk about it later."

I cross my arms over my chest. "We will?"

Asher closes his eyes and takes a deep breath. "Yes. I don't want to fight. I just—I don't want to have this conversation here, in front of everyone. Can we hang out for a bit, have our dance, and then figure things out from there?"

I exhale slowly. "Yeah. That's—okay."

He shoots me a tentative smile, and when I send him an answering one, he darts forward and pecks a kiss to my cheek.

Heat rushes through me at the innocent contact. It's nothing—not at all a big deal.

But it's everything.

He pulls out a seat, ushering me into it, then settles next to me. To my surprise, Asher reaches for my hand again, pulling it into his and squeezing my fingers.

"You look gorgeous," he murmurs. "Did I mention that?"

I swallow. "No." My voice is a hoarse whisper.

"You took my breath away," he whispers. "When I saw you sitting there…"

"Yeah?"

"I'm glad you're here," he says with finality.

I shiver.

"Cold?" he asks.

I shake my head.

But he's already slipping out of his tux jacket. He drapes it around my shoulders, enveloping me in his rich scent of winter and apple pie spice.

"There you go," he murmurs, before he tucks his arm around my shoulders and draws me into his side.

My eyes fall closed, and I let myself indulge in the fantasy. I know Asher's a physically affectionate guy, that's his love language, but when he touches me like this, I almost start to believe...

Maybe Elliott was right. Maybe I wasn't out of line for thinking he might return my feelings.

On my left, Yoni asks Asher a question, and on my right, Elise and Kate are chatting with their dates, and I...

I'm sitting here, wearing Asher's tux jacket, his arm wrapped around my shoulders. Shifting my chair, I angle a little closer to him, so there's less strain on his shoulder, and he tightens his arm around me. The faint smile he sends me warms me thoroughly.

I don't know what this is. I don't know that I *want* to know what this is.

With Asher distracted by Yoni and Elliott, I reach into my clutch for my phone. Sadie and Rachel knew my plans—they had to, they convinced me to show up, and they helped me pick out my dress.

Nobody else knows.

So I'm surprised when I see a text from Estee, my best friend from home.

**Estee**: *How was it seeing Asher?*

I freeze. How did she know? *What* does she know?

A second text pops up on my phone display.

**Estee**: *He said he ran into you at a bar. You? At a bar? On a Monday night?*

With a breath of laughter, I relax.

**Arielle**: *Just a rough day at work. Off-season prep is no joke.*

**Estee**: *So??? How was it?*

She's pressing. Why? She and Asher have always had a weird relationship. Sometimes they act like best friends, and other times they go months without talking.

**Arielle**: *How was what?*

**Estee**: *Seeing him. Is it weird? He's been quiet since we all met up, and then this week, he started texting me again.*

I pause. Monday night's flight from the bar feels like a year ago.

But he's texting Estee.

My best friend.

He's been talking to her all this time.

**Arielle**: *What else did he say? Do you guys talk a lot?*

Asher looks my way, quirks a smile, then turns back to Elliott.

**Estee**: *More in the last week than we have in the last two years. I've missed him.*

My stomach sinks.

I've read this wrong.

I've read this situation all wrong.

Hurt prickles at the back of my eyes, and I exhale slowly to keep myself from letting the tears fall.

How stupid was I to fall for this? For him?

And for him to be chatting up Estee this whole time...

I push back my chair. As much as I want to enjoy the moment, the simple comfort of his presence, it's been tainted. I take off Asher's jacket and grab my clutch and wrap.

"What's up?" He asks.

I shake my head. "I need some air."

He looks confused. "Arielle..."

"I'll be okay," I tell him. "Don't worry about me."

*He never has before*, I think to myself.

Tears well in my eyes again, and I turn on my heel and stride towards the ballroom doors.

The coat check is empty—everyone's inside, enjoying the start of the reception. The attendant looks surprised to see me at this point of the wedding. Wordlessly, I hand over my ticket, and when she comes back with my coat, I stuff a few bills in the tip jar.

I don't know how I was so dumb as to fall for this again.

Asher Gold excels at many things, but the one thing he's always done effortlessly is break my heart.

Over and over again, I fall and fall for him, and over and over again, he rips apart any shred of dignity I thought I had. I don't think he even realizes he's doing it.

Hailing a ride-share, I tuck my hands in my pockets and burrow deep into my coat.

Why did I let myself fall for his act?

Why did I let myself think it could ever be real?

I should have known better. Guys like Asher Gold—strong, smart, funny, nice, cute, friendly—aren't interested in girls like me—weird, strange, a little too quiet, a little too shy, a little too... wrong.

No matter what I do, I'm always wrong.

The ride-share car arrives, and after verifying the driver's license plate, I open the car door.

The hotel's doors burst open, and Asher darts out, nearly tripping over the doorman. He stops in his tracks at the sight of me fleeing the scene yet again.

"Arielle," he says, breathless. "Where are you going?"

I take a deep breath and square my shoulders.

"Anywhere that isn't here," I tell him.

And then I duck into the car and close the door behind me.

"You okay?" The driver asks in a thick Southie accent. She's young, about my age, with dark blonde hair and a nose ring. I like her already.

"Just drive."

She eyes me worriedly in the rearview mirror, then pulls into traffic. "You want to talk about him?"

Leaning back against the seat, I sigh. "Want to? No. Should I? Probably."

The driver laughs and shakes her head. "Ah. Been there. Done that. Got the bruises to show for it."

I rub at my suspiciously moist eyes. "Yeah, that's one thing he's always been good at."

# Asher

-------------------------------------------

What in the ever-loving fuck just happened?

One minute, we were fine. We'd had a moment, I introduced her to my friends, I'd even given her my jacket when she was cold! One minute, we were snuggling, and I thought it was almost perfect—if only she knew the truth about how I felt, that would have been the cherry on top.

And then she just... left.

I don't know why. I don't know what I did.

Sitting on the curb with my head in my hands, I take a deep breath, watching as my exhalation puffs up in a cloud in front of me. It's cold out, and the cold of the concrete is already seeping into my bones, numbing me on the outside to match my already numb heart.

*Anywhere that isn't here*, she said.

Why? What did I do?

I don't think she was overstimulated. She didn't seem tense. She seemed *fine*.

I could ask her friends, but I don't know that they'd give me a ~~second third~~ fourth chance.

Fuck. I just wish I knew how to fix this. I wish I knew what I did to *cause* this.

With a sigh, I stand and make my way back into the hotel, slipping into the back of the ballroom. I debate getting a drink, but I know that given my mood, I'd probably overindulge. I don't have the strength to watch my tolerance right now.

Elliott approaches. "You okay, babe?" they ask.

We've been over for three years, but they've always called me babe. It's not romantic, it signifies my presence in their inner circle. We're better as friends than as lovers.

"I'm fine," I say automatically.

They snort.

"Okay, I'm fucking confused. I have no idea what just happened."

"She needs some space," Elliott tells me.

"Did she tell you what happened?"

They shake their head. "Not specifically."

Anxiety grips me. "What did she say?"

"Just that she was sorry to duck out early, but she didn't feel it was appropriate given the circumstances." Their mouth twists in distaste. "I have no idea what that means. She was fine all through the ceremony. Didn't seem to have an issue in the cocktail hour. It's only been, what, half an hour?"

I ransack my mind trying to put the pieces together.

"Have you told her yet?"

Shaking my head, I run my hand through my hair. "I asked her to dance with me. I was going to tell her then."

"Oh, babe." Elliott pats my shoulder.

"It's like her Bat Mitzvah all over again. We were going to dance, and then—"

I stop.

My eyes rise to Elliott's.

"We were going to dance, and then when the song came on, she was nowhere to be found."

"Go get her," they say urgently. "Bring her back, or fuck, stay with her. But don't let her get away. Not again."

Nodding quickly, I pat my pockets to make sure I have everything. "Tell Yoni I'm sorry for ducking out, too. I'll text Alex and Mara and apologize. I gotta—"

I take a deep breath.

"You gotta get your girl," Elliott tells me with a slow grin.

"Yeah. I need my girl."

"You're going to get her," they tell me. They pull me in for a tight hug. "I'm so proud of you."

"Don't be proud yet," I warn. "She still has to say yes."

"Are you proposing?"

My insides seize up. "No?" I choke.

But... I kind of want to.

I know, logically, we have so many things to discuss before then. Marriage is a contract, it's a legally binding life change, but...

I want it.

I want it *with Arielle*.

Nobody else.

"As long as you don't bring her a ring tonight, I think she'll say yes to anything you ask," Elliott says. They clap my shoulder. "Now go get her."

Scurrying through the hotel lobby, I call a ride-share, and it arrives by the time I've gotten my coat and made my way outside.

"I'll double your rate if you can get me to Medford in ten minutes or less," I tell the driver.

He's a middle-aged man with a potbelly and a cigarette behind his ear. "That's a twenty-five minute drive on a good day."

"I just need to get there," I tell him. "I need to get to her."

He eyes me curiously. "So there's a girl?"

Quickly, I nod.

"I'll go as fast as I can," he promises.

Buckling my seatbelt, I am thrown back against the backrest as he pulls into traffic and zooms forward.

He doesn't get me to Medford in ten minutes.

But he manages it in fourteen.

"Thanks, man," I tell him. "I'll take care of you."

"Anything for love," he says.

I blink. Love.

*Love.*

I love her. I am one hundred percent in love with Arielle Weiss.

Running down the stairs, I make my way to the basement-level entrance to her apartment.

I ring the doorbell, and when she doesn't answer in three seconds, I ring it again. And again.

The door is wrenched open, and I'm greeted by the sight of the most beautiful woman in the world.

Arielle has washed off her makeup and pulled her curls into a ponytail. Fresh-faced, her eyes are red—nearly as red as the crimson pajamas she's wearing.

"What are you doing here?" she asks.

"What the hell happened?" I demand.

"You should go," she says.

"Arielle..." I move towards her, and she edges the door shut. I stop in my tracks. "Little Lion, tell me. What did I do?"

Her mouth twists. "Maybe you should ask Estee."

I blink a few times, processing. *What?*

"Like... Estee Cohen? From our Hebrew school class?" I'm so confused. Estee and I have been friends since we were in diapers—our moms met in a baby group before we were even born.

She nods.

"I don't know what you're talking about. Estee and I are friends."

Arielle scoffs. "Not the way she tells it."

"I love Estee," I tell her.

Her face falls.

"But I'm *in love* with you."

Arielle stares at me.

"What?" she breathes.

"I'm in love with you," I tell her. "I thought we were—I wanted to dance with you, and I was going to tell you then, and... I'm in love with you."

"Asher." Her voice is pained. "I can't."

"Is it because of Trevor?"

It's her turn to blink. "What? No."

"Because when I tried to kiss you back home—"

"I broke up with him," she says. "We were together for two and a half years, and the day I got back from Chicago, I dumped him."

"Then why..." My mind reels.

"Because that night, I wanted you to kiss me," Arielle says.

I swallow. "Just that night?"

She exhales slowly. "And every night since."

"So then why did you leave? We were—we could—"

"You don't have feelings for Estee?" she asks again.

I shake my head. "Arielle, it's you. It's only you."

"When we were kids, I had a crush on you," she blurts.

It's my turn to exhale. What?

"And tonight when I got that text from Estee, the only thing I could think about is that time when I finally worked up the courage to ask you to junior formal, you told me you were going to the dance with her."

My stomach sinks. "So this just pushed you back into that head-space?"

I know high school was rough for her. She didn't really date—not until college. She was too shy. Too withdrawn. It's only been in the last few years that I've really seen her blossom into the slightly more confident version of herself that I've seen the last few days.

Tentatively, Arielle nods. "It took me six months to work up the courage to ask you out. I was convinced tonight would be the night. I would—I planned—"

She breaks off with a groan. She looks up at me.

"I wanted to. I was going to make this grand gesture, and then—"

"I liked seeing you there. I want you to get to know my friends, and I want to meet yours, and—I want our worlds to merge. I want our whole lives to merge."

Her eyes widen.

"I want it. I want you. And I know we have some things to talk about, but I want to make it clear—I want forever with you. This isn't some fling. This isn't a passing fancy. This is the real thing. You and me..."

I take a step forward, and when she doesn't close the door, I reach for her hand with my gloved one.

"Arielle, I want *you*."

She swallows nervously. "Ash..."

I squeeze her hand. "Can I come in?"

Nodding quickly, Arielle releases my hand and opens the door wider. Inside, I shuck my scarf, coat, and gloves. She takes them from me, hanging it up and tucking the gloves into the pocket.

Stepping forward, I draw her into my arms.

"I've been wanting to do this all night," I tell her.

She bites her lip. "Me, too."

A small smile crosses my face, and I reach up and pull her lip free. Her soft gasp puffs against my skin, and a shiver runs down my spine.

"I love you," I whisper. "I'm in love with you."

"Asher, I..."

Laying my index finger against her lips, I shake my head. "It's not a competition. I don't want you to say it until it's real."

"But—"

"You don't have to say it," I insist.

Arielle scowls up at me. "Will you shut the hell up and kiss me already?"

# Arielle

---

A sher Gold was my first kiss. It was a dare, spurred on by a game of Spin the Bottle when we were sixteen, but I've never forgotten it.

Now, at twenty-six, I want Asher Gold to be my last kiss.

When he slides his mouth over mine, a whole-body glow warms me from my toes to my eyelashes.

My arms slide around his neck, and he sighs, pulling me closer, his lips teasing mine.

This is nothing like our first kiss ten years ago. This is nothing like the peck he gave my cheek an hour ago.

This is...

Fire.

His hand is an icicle on my cheek, his skin freezing from the chilly temperatures outside. It's a stark, tangible reminder, grounding me. It keeps me from falling even deeper.

Asher loves me.

Asher *loves* me.

This is all I've wanted since that night at Cole's bar back home in Chicago. When he flirted with me and hugged on me and generally treated me like I was the center of his whole world.

The long forgotten crush flared back to the forefront of my mind, and it's been toying with me the last few weeks. I spent the plane ride home writing my speech, but when I met up with my now ex at the diner across from his office, what came out was:

"I'm not interested in continuing this anymore. I've met someone, nothing has happened, but I wanted it to. There was nothing you did or could have done."

And Trevor—sweet, kind, rather oblivious Trevor—just sighed. "It was him, wasn't it?"

"Who?"

"The guy from your hometown," he'd said. "The one you ran into at the grocery store and spent an hour and a half talking with in the dairy aisle."

And now...

Yeah, it's always been him. It's always been Asher. He's been the one constant in my life.

No matter where I've been in my life, I've always known he was my friend.

No matter how overwhelmed I've been, I've always known he would drop everything to help me.

No matter how many people are around, I've always known him to give me his undivided attention.

No matter what's going on with us, I've always known I could rely on him.

And as he stands there holding me in his arms, kissing me, saying all the things I've wanted to hear for so long... I have to pinch myself.

The sharp pain on the inside of my wrist makes me jump.

Asher pulls back, his hands moving squarely on my hips. "Are you okay?" He's breathless, his cheeks pink, his mouth swollen.

"What are we doing?" I ask.

He cocks his head at me. "Um..."

"Not the kissing." I wave my hand in the air. "What is this?"

"What do you want it to be?" he asks.

"Don't do that. Don't play games," I snap.

Asher grabs my hand, then drags me across the room to the sofa. He sits down and pulls me beside him, one leg propped between us like a barrier.

"I'm not playing games," he says quietly, meeting my eyes. "I want you. I want to be with you. Do you want to go on a date? Do you want to be my girlfriend? Do you want to move in with me? Do you want to get married?"

I inhale sharply.

"Because, honey, I'm not opposed to any of that. We've known each other for so long," Asher tells me. "There are things we should talk about if we want to get married—I want my brother to be there, and I'm guessing you want your parents and Simon—but fuck it, let's do it next weekend, I'm game if you are."

My breath catches in my throat. "What?" My voice comes out squeaky and high-pitched.

Asher takes my hand in his, rubbing his thumb over my knuckles. "And if you want to go on a date, or a year or three of dates, I can do that, too. I want to be up front with you on what I want. So, Arielle, what do *you* want?"

And for the first time... I consider it. I never thought this would ever happen. I hoped, sure, but I didn't think it would ever realistically come true.

So what do I want? What do I *need*?

"I don't want to get married," I finally say.

Asher nods gamely. "Ever?"

"Next weekend." I force a laugh. "Maybe... we try dating for a bit."

Agreeable, he nods again. "Yes. I like this. Yes."

"My lease is up in September."

"Great, so we'll table the apartment searching until this summer," he says.

I rub at my forehead. "Is this crazy? This is crazy."

"It might be," Asher says.

I stare at him.

"But that doesn't change the fact that it feels *right*."

His words sit heavy between us.

He's right.

It feels so right. So natural. Like fate.

Standing, I brush imaginary lint off my pajamas to cover my nerves.

Asher hurries to his feet. "I'll let you get some rest. I'll—"

"I want you to stay." I exhale. "I want you to stay, and I—"

"Whatever you want," he's quick to reassure me.

Taking him by the hand, I pull him across the small living room to my bedroom, the second door on the right.

"Bathroom's through there, I share it with Rachel," I report. "Sadie's on the other side of the kitchen."

"I like your apartment," he says, and I laugh, because all he's seen is the grey walls of the hallway.

"I like you in my apartment," I tell him.

Pulling him into my room, I close the door behind us and push him gently towards the unmade bed.

Asher looks around the room, taking in the messy puddle of throw blankets on the floor and the pile of clean laundry I've yet to put away on my desk chair. He toes off his dress shoes and takes off his tux jacket before he sits on the side of my bed, staring guilelessly up at me.

"What do you want?" he whispers.

I want—

I want—

*I want.*

This is the first time I've ever felt want and need this intense.

This is Asher. This is the guy I've known for so long... Our friendship has ebbed and flowed over the last twenty years, but there's no denying he's been there for so many of my formative memories. He was part of so many formative experiences. He...

My eyes fall closed and, taking a deep breath, I lift my pajama shirt over my head.

I'm not wearing a bra.

"Holy shit," he breathes.

Self-conscious, I cross my arms over my chest.

"Arielle..." He reaches for me, pulling my hands free. "Little Lion, you're absolutely gorgeous."

"You're just saying that," I deflect.

Asher shakes his head. "I'm not. Babe, I'm not. If you knew how long I've been thinking about this..."

My eyes dart to his.

"A very long time," Asher says seriously. He tugs me toward him.

I move to straddle his lap, but to my surprise, he lays back on my bed, pulling me alongside him until we're stretched out, our heads on my pillows.

His hand lands on my bare hip, and when I shiver, he slides it up and up and up, cupping my breast. His kiss is light, exploratory.

Slowly, I unfurl, reaching for him. My hands work at the buttons on his dress shirt, pulling the starched white shirt away.

Asher pulls back a bit and helps. Sitting up, he works the shirt off his broad shoulders, revealing a tight white undershirt. A tuft of curly dark chest hair is visible above the v-neck, and I lean forward, pressing a kiss there. He groans.

"Ari..."

I reach for his shirt, and he helps me, lifting the white cotton shirt over his head.

Asher—he's *thick*, and I absolutely love it. He's always been a bit on the stocky side, wide and broad, and that hasn't changed. He's got a nice layer of fluff surrounding his lightly-furred belly, and when I reach out to run my fingers through the happy trail leading down to his pants, he holds his breath.

He stops my hand when I reach his belt.

"We're not doing this," he says.

I pout. "Really?"

"Nope." He kisses me lightly.

"But I want you to fuck me."

"I don't want to fuck you," Asher says.

Hurt, I rear back.

"I want to love you," he continues. "There will be a time and a place for us to take the next step, and it will make sense, but tonight? I don't want to rush this."

I let out a hollow laugh. "You practically proposed marriage half an hour ago."

He cracks a smile. "Yeah, and we agreed to take it a bit slower, so we don't need to rush."

"So if I were to take off my pants right now..."

"Yes. Please, do," he nods readily. His hand moves to cup my core over my pajamas. "I want you to feel good."

"I always feel good when I'm with you," I say quietly.

I feel very small all of a sudden. Asher has always had this enormous presence, and I'm just me.

What on earth does he see in me?

When is he going to realize everything else that's out there for him?

He can have anyone. Why is he wasting his time with me?

"Hey." He trails his thumb down my cheek. "Where'd you go?"

I bite my lip.

"Are your thoughts too loud? Do you need me to distract you?" He traces my lip with the same thumb. "Talk to me. Tell me what's going on."

"I just..." I blow out a breath.

How do I say this? How do I reveal all my deepest insecurities?

In one fluid movement, Asher moves down the bed. His fingers curl into my flannel pajama pants and slowly ease them down.

I hold my breath. He taps my hip, and I lift up for him to pull them further down.

The pants are halfway down my thighs when he pauses, then lowers his head.

My cunt is exposed, and he presses a kiss to the hood of my clit before ducking his chin lower. His fingers work the fabric further as his mouth expertly explores my body.

Kicking away the pants, I let out a sigh of relief when I'm free of the fabric, and Asher moves further down, spreading my legs and revealing me to him.

I want to be shy. I want to hide. I want to run away.

But the look on his face...

"You're gorgeous," he whispers. He spreads me, revealing the hard nub of my clit. With a sigh, he lowers his mouth to me, sucking hard.

My heart stops beating.

My hips come off the bed.

"Absolutely fucking gorgeous," he says firmly, before he lifts two fingers to his mouth. He sucks on them for a moment, then resumes his exploration of my pussy.

He traces a wet line up my soaking slit. One of his spit-slicked fingers eases inside of me, and my back arches, and he smiles against my cunt.

The rough hairs of his short beard provide an exquisite kind of friction between my hairless thighs. When I had the idea to crash the wedding, I booked an emergency bikini wax, and I'm so fucking thankful I did. I'm not opposed to a little body hair, but I wouldn't want anything to get between us in the moments it matters most.

My hands fall to his head, carding my fingers through his curls, and he groans, adding a second finger inside me and twisting his wrist.

I gasp, locking my legs around his head. He increases the pressure on my clit, scraping his teeth along the sensitive bud, then sucking away the sting.

Asher pulls away, and before I can stop myself, I let out a whine.

His cheeks are flushed, his mouth slick and swollen.

"Do you use toys?" he asks.

I flush.

And because I'm naked, he knows now that my flush travels all the way down my chest.

He scrapes his teeth over one of my nipples, pinching the other.

"Toys?" he asks again.

"Um…"

"If you don't like them, that's okay. I'll just zig instead of zag."

I cover my face with my hands. "I can't believe you're asking me what I use to get myself off."

"Next time, at my place, I'll happily show you what I have on hand," he says with a smirk.

"Oh, I'm sure you would." I sift my fingers through his curls. "You've always been fearless."

He shrugs. "Sex and desire don't embarrass me. There's no reason for it to make you uncomfortable."

"I'm not used to verbalizing what I want," I admit.

Asher grins. "Oh, that's going to change."

# Asher

-------------------------------------------------

Arielle finally points me towards her toys, and—well, she has quite the collection. She's not nearly as innocent as she pretends.

I like it.

Picking out a vibrator with a rabbit attachment, I slick it with the lube and test the buzz on the lowest setting. Her mouth falls open, and she watches with bated breath as I press the silicone wand to the inside of her thigh.

She jumps.

"Relax," I murmur, before I kiss her neck.

Arielle sighs, running her fingers through my hair again.

Teasing her, I move the slick, vibrating wand to the apex of her thighs, then down the inside of her other leg. She whines.

"Ash..." Her breath hitches. "Please," she says softly.

Propping myself up on my elbow, I look down at her delicious body, splayed out for me like a feast.

"You don't like teasing?" I ask.

"Not right now." Her hand on my cheek directs my mouth back to hers, and she takes control of the kiss, licking into my mouth and devouring the taste of herself on my lips.

I move the vibrator to the slick slit of her cunt, then draw it up to press against her sensitive bud.

Arielle jerks, then sighs, relaxing her body as the vibrations make their way through her.

Her soft breath against my cheek is coming quicker now. Her hands can't stop touching me, mapping my shoulders and chest, raking her fingers through my chest hair, scratching her nail over my nipple, and I—

I can't think.

I want to bring *her* pleasure. This isn't about me. This is about her.

Slowly, I tease the vibrator around her opening, and Arielle cants her hips up. I ease the thick, bulbous head inside of her, letting her get used to the intrusion.

"Ash," she whispers.

I fucking love it when she calls me that.

"More?" I ask quietly.

She bites her lip and nods, her eyes locked on mine.

"I need words, babe."

"No words. More." She arches her back, trying to pull the toy inside of her. "Need..."

With one smooth thrust, I ease the vibrator all the way inside of her, so the flexible silicone rabbit ears are pressed flush against her clit.

Arielle gasps, and I swallow it with a kiss. She moans and wraps her arms around my neck, trying to draw me closer.

I shift until I'm half laying on top of her, with her neck laying on my bicep, our top halves pressed flush together.

Her fingers scrabble for me. Her short, unpolished nails scratch down my back when I draw the vibrator out and then back inside, then again, and again, and again.

As her hips ride the toy, her eyes fall closed. Her head tilts back.

I lean down and kiss my way down her neck. I have to shift her slightly to get any further, and I suck her gorgeous tit into my mouth, tonguing the rough, pebbled bud of her nipple.

When I bite down gently, Arielle groans.

"Like that?" I murmur, moving to the other.

She nods quickly. "Ash, I need—" She grunts, arching her back.

"Good?"

"Top," she pants.

"Stop?"

"Don't stop. Don't," she says, breathless. "I need—*unh.*"

Her hands clutch at my shoulders. Her nails dig little half-moons into my skin.

I hope she leaves marks. I hope they stay. I would give everything I have to be branded permanently hers.

For a sprightly little thing, she sure is strong. Before long, she manhandles me until more of my body weight is laying over her. My cock is hard, aching, pressed against the side of her hip.

But this isn't about me.

Arielle maneuvers until I'm hovering over her, then she wraps her legs around my waist and drives her hips up, her heels digging into the backs of my thighs. With every thrust, our chests brush against one another, and she arches her back, trying to get closer.

She kisses me—hard, demanding. With one hand on my shoulder, the other slides down to my ass, pulling me down on top of her.

"Babe—I don't—" I'm a big guy, and she's significantly smaller than me.

"Need—pressure," she pants. "Please--"

Dropping lower, I try to keep my weight off of her, and she pulls me into her again.

When she gets overstimulated, when the outside world gets to be too much, physical pressure helps calm her nervous system. It's like with hugs; she wants the intensity of strong pressure, or she can't deal.

And that's when I realize—she needs that physical pressure now to ground her, to orient herself. She needs to be able to focus on the pleasure, not on everything else going on.

So when I start to rest my body weight on her, and she moans long and loud, I smile against her lips and increase the speed of the vibrator, before kissing my way back down the column of her neck.

Arielle rides the toy, her hips working against my pelvis, seeking her pleasure. When I reach the spot beneath her ear, she tenses.

With a gasp, she throws her head back. Grunts.

And then she makes the most beautiful sound I've ever heard, announcing her pleasure.

I don't stop my rhythm, thrusting the toy against her clit to prolong her release. She screws her eyes shut tight.

"Ash," she breathes, melting into the mattress. Her hips slow, lazily working the vibrator. I turn the speed down to the first level, bringing her back down.

Her legs loosen around me, sliding down to wrap loosely around my lower body. She raises one arm above her head, running it through her curls. Arielle sighs, spent and content.

When I'm certain she's done, I turn off the vibrator and ease it out of her, tossing it to the side. I can feel her wetness seeping into the fabric of my pants.

It's a fucking badge of honor.

She looks like a goddess, her skin flushed, her lips swollen, her pupils lust-blown.

"How do you feel?" I ask, trailing a hand over her hair.

"Mm. Good," she says, fluttering her eyes open, then closed again. "I think you killed me."

"That's not good," I tell her lightly. "I'm not into necrophilia."

She pauses, then opens her eyes and looks at me curiously. I see her mouth the word *necrophilia*.

And then she giggles. She giggles again. And then she bursts into uncontrollable laughter.

I did that. Me. I made her laugh.

I want to do it all the fucking time.

Holding her in my arms... I've never felt this content, this comfortable. My hand rubs up and down her arm, memorizing the softness of her skin, the little mole on the inside of her elbow, the freckles on her shoulder.

When she's had enough cuddling, Arielle squirms away, and I roll over, scooping my shirt off the floor.

"Where are you—" She cuts off. "What are you doing?"

"Getting dressed," I say easily.

"Oh. Are you going back to the wedding?" She blinks at me a few times.

"No. Honey, no, I'm not leaving." I sit down on the edge of her bed, reaching for her again.

"Then why are you putting on your clothes?"

I scratch at my clavicle, confused.

"Don't you want to..." She mimes jerking off, her eyes locked on my crotch.

My dick wants to, yes. I would love to. But my heart's already won this battle; it always has, where she's concerned.

"I wanted to get you there," I say instead. "There's no hurry."

"But you didn't get to come." Arielle pouts. "That doesn't seem fair."

"In a relationship, it's not a 50:50 ratio of who gets to come."

She raises her eyebrows, crossing her arms over her chest. "It's not?"

"Nope." I grin at her. "For every one of mine, I expect you to have at least three, if not four."

"Oh." Arielle looks taken aback. "So you don't want to?"

"Later." I duck down and kiss her forehead. "It gives me something to look forward to."

She smiles softly, fisting my t-shirt and pulling me down to kiss me.

Grabbing my tuxedo shirt off the floor, I toss it to her. "How do you feel about a midnight snack?"

She cocks her head to the side, slipping her arms into my shirt.

"I don't know," she says. "It's only ten-thirty."

It's my turn to laugh. "Okay, how about a ten-thirty snack?"

"Is there cheese involved?" she asks seriously.

"With you involved? Yes, honey, there will be cheese." I wink at her. "Did you think I've forgotten your five favorite food groups?"

Arielle frowns. "Cheese, wine... what else?"

"Cheese and moscato," I tick off on my fingers. "Chocolate, everything bagels, and pickles. Maybe chicken piccata, but I still think pickles will win that fight."

She smiles at me, slightly awed. "You remember."

"I remember everything about you," I tell her. I offer my hand. "Come on. Snack, then we can get you ready for round two."

"What's round two?" She dips to slip on her pajama pants, then buttons up my shirt.

"I don't know if you remember this about me, but I'm very adept at cuddling." I wink again, and I'm rewarded when she giggles.

"Yeah, I remember." Her cheeks tint pink.

"We're going to cuddle, and we're going to hang out, and talk, and maybe make out," I tell her easily. "We get to be together. There's nothing keeping us apart anymore."

Arielle reaches for my hand. "I like this."

"Good. I'm glad." I kiss her forehead again. "Get used to it."

# Arielle

---------------------------------------------------

## Sunday, Night 6

Asher and I laze in bed most of Sunday morning, until he has to leave for the after-wedding brunch. He invited me to join him, but I don't think I can face his friends knowing I ran out of their wedding because I got insecure over a non-issue. So he kissed me goodbye, went home to shower, and went to join his friends.

About five minutes after he left, my roommates barged into my room.

"What the fuck," Sadie says, perching on my desk chair.

"That sounded intense," Rachel adds.

"What did?"

"The two-hour fucking session last night?" Rach says, her eyebrows raised.

"We didn't fuck," I use her words. "We just..."

Sadie smirks at me. "Yeah?"

"He's a very aggressive cuddler," I finally say.

She laughs. "If by aggressive you mean—"

"Really talented with his fingers, and his mouth, and toys." I blush. "Several times over."

After our snack, we had round two... and that turned into a round three for me.

"Yeah. Get it, girl," Sadie holds her hand up for a high five.

"You won't hear me complaining." I can't hide my smile. It feels like it's stretching from ear to ear, splitting my face in two.

"So? What now?" Rach asks.

"What do you mean?"

"When are you going to see him again?" She demands.

"Oh. I don't know." I glance at my phone screen. I have a text from him already, on the T back to his place, and it makes me smile. "He didn't mention it."

"But you're going to see him again?" Sadie pushes.

Quickly, I nod. "He told me he loves me."

Her eyes light up and she clasps her hands under her chin. "He did?"

I flush. "He actually suggested we get married. Next weekend."

My friends blink in unison and look at each other.

"And?" Rachel demands.

"And I said, let's try dating first." I shrug, trying to hide both how happy and uncomfortable I am at the same time. "I mean..."

"He *proposed*?" Sadie repeats.

"He even knew that I'd want my parents and my brother there, and he'd want his brother, and..." I bite my lip. "I'm not going to. Obviously. We need to figure this out."

"Figure what out?" Rach says. "He loves you, and you obviously adore him. What else is there?"

"Well... can we sustain a relationship, for one," I point out. "We need to make sure we're compatible before we embark on a legal contract like marriage."

Sadie rolls her eyes. "Marriage is about more than legal contracts."

"At its core—" I start.

"No. It's about love," she insists, ever the romantic.

"We have a lot to talk about," I tell her simply. "We should make sure we align on certain things."

"Like?" Rachel raises her eyebrows.

"Well, future plans. Career. Family. Lifestyle." I chew the inside of my cheek. "I don't know if I want to move back to Chicago. What if he wants to? Can I stand in the way of that?"

"Or maybe he just wants to be wherever you are," Sadie suggests.

"Yeah, maybe..." I shrug. "Either way, it's a lot to discuss. We don't have to figure it out on day one. And we should probably make sure we're compatible in bed, first."

"You certainly seemed... *compatible*," Rachel teases.

I clear my throat. "We didn't... consummate."

Sadie looks at me pointedly. "You didn't?"

"I wanted to. He said something about ratios and not being interested. He barely let me touch him."

Rachel looks murderous. She pushes her sweater sleeves up her arms. "He said that?"

"I'm confused. You say that like it's a bad thing?" I tilt my head, surveying her. "Isn't it a good thing that he wants me to get off, more than he cares about it for himself?"

She stares at me, her mouth moving like a fish out of water. "Wait—"

"He wasn't body shaming her," Sadie tells her. "He was talking about the ratio of orgasms."

"Ohhhhh." Rachel sags against the dresser. "Okay. He can live, then."

I laugh. "Were you about to commit homicide for me again?"

"Anything you for, babe," she teases, winking at me.

"Aw. I'm touched." I grin at her.

"Lunch?" Sadie asks. "And I could use a trip to the bookstore..."

I roll my eyes. "Sure. Lemme shower first, though."

***

## Monday, Night 7

After a much overdue girls' day, it's back to business as usual. Asher didn't come back after the brunch—our texting conversation was interrupted by a call from his brother, and knowing how infrequently they get to talk to each other, I let him go with a promise to see each other the next night at his work holiday party. It's final exam time, so he's busy marking tests and finishing up grades, but his fellow teachers have arranged an evening out at a local brewery.

I show up a little past six in dark jeans and a cute sweater. My roommates and I lit the candles before I left—it's already the seventh night. Chanukah is almost over.

Asher is in the center of a group of people, and he stops in the middle of his conversation at the sight of me. A grin stretches from ear to ear. Darting forward, he crosses the pub and makes his way to me. He pauses, then tugs me into a tight, firm hug.

"Hey, baby," he breathes, holding me securely. "I didn't know if you'd make it."

"I'd go anywhere for you," I admit.

As much as I hate crowds, as much as I dislike strangers, as much as I can't stand being fake-social... if he asked me to do it? I'd volunteer, and then do it again, just to see his smile.

He kisses me softly. "I know it's not the same as a real date," he says quietly. "You deserve the conventional, you know, dinner and—"

"I love it," I interrupt. "It's perfect for us."

It's how this started, a night out at the bar. It doesn't need to be fancy and frilly and uptight. It can be just *us*.

"C'mon. Let me introduce you," he says, taking my hand.

Asher teaches seventh grade social studies at a nearby charter school. He always knew he wanted to be a teacher—in high school, he volunteered at Hebrew school with the younger kids, helping as an aide in their classes. In college, he ran the preteen youth group at the local synagogue. He's fun and easygoing. I can see why the kids like him.

And it's easy to see why his fellow teachers like him, too. He's just so... Asher. Charming and laid-back, and effortlessly confident. He's comfortable in his skin.

Sometimes, I hate how jealous of him I am. Nothing seems to phase him; nothing seems to bother him for long. Not his parents' terrible treatment of his brother, or my parents' awful treatment of me, or—

He presses a kiss to my temple, then introduces me to his friends and peers. There are so many names and faces, I don't have a hope of remembering, and I don't think he's counting on me to, either. I make a note of his boss, Gloria, and her wife, but all the others blur into a cacophony that makes my head hurt.

All I know is Asher is holding my hand, and he doesn't seem like he's about to let it go anytime soon.

I like that. I like that a lot.

So when my phone vibrates and I have a text from Estee, my stomach sinks. I haven't forgiven myself for the moment of insecurity when I found out they'd been talking again. I doubted him, I doubted her, I doubted myself.

**Estee**: *Ash says the two of you have a Chanukah present for me. What is it??*

I poke his arm and show him the text.

He smiles, then kisses my knuckles. "I thought you could tell her."

"You want to tell people?"

Asher laughs. "Babe, I want to shout it from the rooftops. Want me to hire a skywriter? Maybe I can put it on the big screen at TD Garden."

With a laugh of my own, I shove his shoulder lightly, then let him pull me in for a hug. He kisses my temple.

"I'll take your lead," he says. "Honestly, I was talking about the marshmallow penguins we saw at the craft fair. But if you want to tell her..."

I smile at him, then lean up for a kiss. "I think you should tell her."

He rubs his nose against mine, before meeting me for a soft kiss.

"How about we tell her together?" He suggests.

"I like the sound of that."

# Asher

------------------------------------------------

## Tuesday, Night 8

It's the last night of Chanukah, but it feels like the beginning.
It's our first real date—just me and Arielle, no party-crashers, no
interlopers, no pretenses. Just us.

We had a good time at my work party last night, but we didn't get a
chance to be *alone*. There were coworkers everywhere, and every time
I tried to take a moment for just us, someone came to interrupt us.

Everyone wanted to meet Arielle—and I can hardly blame her. I've
been talking about her for the last few months, trying to work up
the nerve to initiate something, anything, between us. And this last
week... nobody's been shy on commenting about the fact that I've
been extraordinarily happy at work, even in the midst of our worst
week of the term (final exams and grading).

But tomorrow is my last day of work before a two and a half week
break, and I know Arielle has some down time in her schedule with

the baseball team being off season. Maybe we can hole ourselves up in one of our apartments and never leave.

There's a knock on my door shortly past six, and I rush to answer the door before my roommate Benji can barge in and hijack the conversation.

Arielle is standing on the doorstep, wearing a dark red wool coat and a white knit scarf and hat. Her cheeks are pink and her eyes are bright. She checks me out, and I can feel my face heat at the sparkle in her eye.

"Hi," she says, a little bit breathless.

Wordlessly, I tug her hand, pulling her into the apartment. Before I even take off her warm winter gear, I'm pulling her into my arms and kissing her.

"How was your day?" I ask, like we haven't been texting all day long.

"It was okay." She shrugs, unbuttoning her coat. "I was talking to this guy."

"Oh?" I hang her coat up on the hook next to mine. "Do you like him?"

"Not really," she says, tilting her head to study me.

My stomach sinks. Maybe she wasn't talking about me after all. Maybe she—

"In fact," she says blandly, "I think I might love him."

My eyes snap to hers. "What?"

"I think I might be in love with this guy," Arielle continues. "He's nice and charming, and he always puts my needs first, and while I know that might get irritating after a while, right now it's really nice."

My throat feels like sandpaper. "It is?"

"I'm acknowledging it's a bit of a honeymoon period right now," she says. "But that doesn't mean it's not enjoyable. It really is. And I'm not rushing—I'm taking it one step at a time."

Hope blooms within me. "But you... love him?"

She bites her lip, bottom. "I really think I do," she says quietly.

"Arielle..." I reach for her, and she falls into my arms, soft and pliant.

"It's you," she whispers. "I'm talking about you."

I hold her tight. "I absolutely adore you."

She smiles. "Good. I'm glad."

She initiates the kiss, taking the lead. Most of the time, it's been me making decisions and running the show—I like that she feels comfortable enough to assert herself with me.

I like that she feels comfortable enough to be herself with me.

There's a loud clapping sound behind us, and we turn to see Benji standing in the doorframe, clapping sarcastically.

"Well done," he says, then he laughs. "You must be the famous Arielle."

"Hi." She tightens her grip on me.

"That's Benji," I say, rolling my eyes. "We went to summer camp together a million years ago. He's an asshole."

"And yet you still put up with me," he says with a snort. "You guys going out?"

The raised eyebrows ask a separate question - are you coming back here for the night?

I nod. "We're headed to dinner."

*And then I'll get my dessert.*

"Wait," Arielle says. "We need to light the candles. It's the last night. My favorite part is seeing all of the candles lit at the same time."

"We can do that," I agree.

"Come on, Benji," Arielle says, a bit stiffly, no inflection in her tone. "Join us."

He squints at me, and I nod. She is being genuine—she's just uncomfortable. Once she settles in and gets to know him, I'm sure we'll all get along well enough. It makes life difficult if your partner and your roommate hate each other.

He lopes over to us and takes out the box of candles from the drawer. The menorah is already on the kitchen counter, along with a box of matches and a knife, which we use to carve out the remnants of the used candle wax each morning.

Busily setting up the candleholder, he carefully orders the candles. It's the end of the box, so our color options are limited, but I know how certain color patterns can set off his OCD. Benji places the candles in a rainbow that works for him, then steps back.

"Would you like to do the honors?" He asks Arielle, holding out the matchbox.

I know there are two reasons he's asking. One, he's trying to be polite—which I appreciate.

The other is that he still can't manage to light a match. Usually, this is my job. It feels sacrilegious to light the Chanukah or Shabbat candles with the same lighter we use to light a joint.

She lights the Shamash, the lead candle, then lights each candle in order from left to right. When she's done, she puts the Shamash back in its holder, and steps back to me. She takes my hand, and I squeeze hers, reveling in the soft magic that she's here, that we're doing this.

Together, the three of us recite the blessings:

First, the *bracha* for the festival of Chanukah: *Baruch atah Adonai, Eloheinu Melech ha'olam, asher kid'shanu b'mitzvotav v'tsivanu l'hadlik ner shel Chanukah*. Second, my favorite prayer, the blessing for the candles themselves: *Baruch atah Adonai, Eloheinu Melech ha'olam, she'asa nissim la'voteinu bayim hahem ba'azman hazeh*.

Arielle turns to me. "We should say the Shehechiyanu."

"You're only obligated to say it on the first night of Chanukah," Benji says.

"But you can also say it on the start of something momentous. And this, us," she squeezes my hand. "This is something new. We're turning a new corner in our friendship."

We've seen each other for a few events together in the last week—the craft fair, the wedding, last night at my work party—but this is the first time Arielle and I are embarking on a real, official date, just the two of us, celebrating and indulging in our fledgling relationship.

It might not work out. We've been friends for so many years, but that doesn't mean the transition to romantic partners will be smooth or easy.

But we have to try. We've come this far; we have to try.

So together, we recite: *Baruch Ata Adonai, Eloheinu Melech ha'olam, shehechiyanu, v'kiy'manu, v'higianu lazman hazeh.*

Blessed are You, Eternal Spirit who has given us life, sustained us, and allowed us to arrive in this moment.

Tears spring to my eyes as the gravity settles in like a weight on my chest. She's right. This is a momentous occasion.

This is the start of the rest of our lives: together, as one, forever intertwined.

I can't fucking wait.

# Arielle

---

When I imagined my first date with Asher Gold, I rather thought it would be... laid back. Chill. Casual. Not—*this*.

He's booked us a table at an exclusive steakhouse in a high-end cluster of the North End neighborhood. There's romantic candlelight and a lady in the corner is playing the harp. He's wearing a suit and a tie, and he looks good enough to eat—I hope I get a chance to, later tonight.

The waiter leads us to our table, nestled in a quiet corner, and I look around curiously. I've never been here—even on a happy hour special, this place is way, *way* out of my price range.

The music is giving me a headache, and the menu doesn't have prices in it. I know that means I probably can't afford to ask what the prices are.

Asher takes my hand. "I know this isn't really... us," he says.

I raise my eyebrows. "Oh?"

"I got caught up in my head," he admits. "I mentioned to some people that we were going for our first real date, and they made all this fuss about making it really special, and now that we're here..." He swallows. "This isn't us, is it?"

Shrugging, I say, "I'd be happy with pizza and beer."

"There will be plenty of that," he promises. "And lots of cheese plates, charcuterie, chicken piccata, and moscato. I thought we might do something a little... special."

I like that he's remembered my favorite foods.

"It's certainly that."

His smile fades. "Do you hate it?"

I squeeze his hand. "Not at all."

"You don't sound enthusiastic," he points out.

"I'm neutral. I neither like nor dislike it." I wave my hand around. "I don't need all of *this*. I just want to be with you. Really, we could have gone to a hockey game, or had a picnic in your living room, or gone to the corner pub. It doesn't need to be fancy."

He doesn't look convinced. This is the first time in ages that I've seen Asher anything but confident.

"It's special because it's us," I tell him. "It's you, and me, and it's us. That's what important. That's what matters."

He doesn't believe me.

"Who were you talking to?"

"My mom," he admits.

My eyes widen. "What did you tell her?"

"That I had a date with the most beautiful girl I've ever met." His cheeks flush, but he holds my gaze. "I didn't give her your name."

My stomach swirls with doubt. Maybe he's changed his mind. Maybe he isn't as serious about this as I thought he was.

"Why not?"

Asher lifts a shoulder. "I figured you'd probably tell your mom first, when you're ready, but I know for sure my mom will tell the whole world, so I wanted the news to get out on your terms, not hers."

That's... surprisingly well thought out.

"Thank you," I tell him quietly, sincerely. "You're always so thoughtful."

He looks away. "Not always."

"Oh?"

"I'm going to mess up. I'm not perfect," Asher says, a little defensively. "I don't want you to put me up on a pedestal. I'm human."

"I know that." His words sting. "Ash, I've known you for so long—I know who you are."

"But you don't, not really. You knew who I was, back when I was a kid. We haven't been friends, really, truly friends, since we went to college halfway across the country from each other."

"And are you suddenly different?" I push back. "Do you treat people like shit?"

His cheeks flush red with anger. "What? No!"

"Do you lie, cheat, or steal?" I demand.

Asher shakes his head. "I'm just..."

"I like *you*," I tell him. I take his hand again. "I like the guy I knew growing up, yes, but I like the man you are today. We might not have spent time together before this week, but—"

"Why didn't we?" He asks. "Were you, like, embarrassed, or...?"

I blink. Open my mouth. Pause.

"Arielle, you never texted me back. I'd initiate plans, and you'd never respond," he says quietly.

"I didn't know how."

It's his turn to blink. "You didn't know how to text back?"

"I didn't know how to blend these two parts of my world." It's hard to put it into words. "I don't... I'm not the same person I was when I was a kid, either. I've figured out more about who I am and what I need—in friendships, in partnerships, in all of it. I was tired of Estee and all of our friends infantilizing me or treating me like I'm fragile. I'm not fragile."

"I know you're not," he says softly. "You're strong. Resilient."

"I can be. Sometimes." I shrug. "I just didn't want to risk crumbling again."

He squints at me.

"It took me a long time to build myself up. It took me a long time to know who I am. I'm more comfortable now. But I was... afraid."

"Of me?" He looks hurt.

I shake my head. "Of *me*. I didn't want to regress." I sigh. "I've finally gotten to this place in my life where I feel mostly confident and comfortable in my skin. I know what my triggers are, I know what I can and can't handle. I just... I wasn't sure I could handle blending the new me with the people who knew the old me."

Asher lets out a heavy breath. "I get that. Really, I do."

I look at him. I look down at the menu.

"You're right," I tell him.

He raises his eyebrows. "Oh?"

"This place is totally not us at all." I laugh. "Let's go."

We haven't ordered—in fact, the waiter has been conspicuously absent. We haven't even been offered drinks yet.

"Go? Go where?"

"It's my turn to surprise you."

Asher stares at me, then suddenly bursts into a sharp laugh.

"Arielle Weiss, you are entirely a surprise," he says, pushing back his chair. He comes around the table and helps me up.

He takes my hand, and I pull him into me, offering a kiss.

There's a light flurry of snow falling as we make our way outside. It's chilly, but not insanely cold.

"Where are we going?" Asher asks.

"You'll see." I smile up at him. I offer my gloved hand, and he takes it in his, letting me lead him down the sidewalk. We're a few blocks away from one of the most famous Italian bakeries in the city. There's usually a mile-long line of people waiting to get in.

What they don't know is that there is a delightful Jewish bakery two blocks over. It's one of those places I never go to purely because of the headache to get to this side of town, but no visit to the North End is complete without a stop at Bubbie Ruth's.

Asher looks at the line outside Matt's Pastry as we pass by. "You wanted to come here?"

Smiling, I shake my head. "Got a better idea."

He grins. "No cannoli? We can have a snack, then play hide the cannoli."

I crack up. "There's cannoli where we're going, too."

His eyebrows knit together as he thinks. There's a half dozen bakeries on this street, none as famous as Matt's.

It isn't until we turn the corner, and Bubbie Ruth's comes into view, that he recognizes where we are.

"I seem to remember eclairs being your favorite dessert," I say, tucking my free hand into my coat pocket. "Bubbie Ruth's has the best eclairs in town."

Asher turns to me, his eyes wide.

He drops my hand.

I flinch.

And then he's pulling me into a hug, squeezing me so tightly I can't breathe.

"You remembered," he says into my ear.

Slowly, I bring my arms up to hug him back. "There's a lot I remember about you."

His eyes are bright as he looks at the door to the bakery, then back at me.

"C'mon," I tell him, taking his hand again. "The cannoli here aren't nearly as good as the cream puffs, but we can do something inventive with pastry cream and whipped cream when we get back to your place."

Asher stops in his tracks. "Fuck, I love you," he says loudly.

My face flames. "You say that now..."

He shakes his head. "I'll say it all the time. I'll say it until you believe it. It's true. It's not about to change."

"Not just because I'm offering to rub pastries on my chest?" I tease.

He laughs. "I mean, that doesn't hurt." He pulls me close again, kissing the tip of my nose. "Let's get the dessert to go, so I can have my fill of you."

"We haven't had dinner yet. We can't eat dessert first."

"Okay, okay," he relents. "We'll get a sandwich, too. You still like a pastrami on rye with Russian dressing?"

Slowly, I nod. "And you still like blintzes with sour cream and cherry preserves?"

Ash shrugs. "What can I say? I love cheese almost as much as you do." He brushes his gloved thumb across my cold cheek, sparking heat along my spine. "But I love you more."

"What the fuck," a loud voice says behind us.

In unison, we turn to face the person on the sidewalk. They're covered head-to-toe in a long coat, a scarf, a hat, and their arms are laden with bags from Matt's Pastry.

"Fucking go inside or move along," the stranger says. "Ugh. Ass-holes." They push past us, striding down the street.

Asher and I turn to each other, then together, we both crack up.

"Come on," I say again, pulling him along beside me. "Let's get you some dessert."

# Asher

- - - - - - - - - - - - - - - - - - - - - - - - - - - - - - - - - - - - - -

Forty-five minutes later, we're walking up the stairs to my apartment. The menorah we lit earlier is visible in the window—Benji must have put it there after we left. He texted me that he was going to sleep early with his noise-cancelling headphones on, so I don't have to worry about keeping quiet.

Jerk. With a laugh, I shake my head. He's a good friend, but he's right; I'm not known for being quiet.

Inside the apartment, we take off our coats and winter gear. Arielle sets the food on the kitchen counter, but before she can untie the bag, I catch her hand and pull her to my room.

"You don't want dinner?" she asks.

"Later," I tell her. "I'm starting with dessert."

Her bright smile takes my breath away.

Closing and locking the door behind me, I toe off my shoes, then loosen my tie.

"So we're doing this?" She asks. Arielle tilts her head. "Just, like... getting down to it?"

Pulling the tie free from my neck, I push her up against the door, then kiss her.

"Just getting comfortable," I tell her, before I lift her into my arms.

She lets out a little shriek, wrapping her arms around my neck, as I walk her to the bed. I deposit her on the mattress, then lean down to unzip her knee-high leather boots. She's wearing fleece tights beneath her fitted dress, and I've scarcely gotten her second boot removed before she's inching the tights down her thick thighs. She stares up at me, lips swollen, hair a mess, her chest rising and falling with her rapid breaths.

"I need you to be naked," she tells me.

I shake my head. "We'll get there."

Arielle cocks her head at me. "Why not now?"

"Because first, I need to have my dessert."

Her cheeks go pink. "The, um, eclairs?"

I shake my head. "You."

She makes an adorable squeaking noise.

And when I join her on the bed, stretching out beside her, she unfolds her tense body and lays next to me. She meets my hungry kiss with eager lips, as if she's even halfway as desperate as I am for this to happen.

I've been thinking about this for a long, long time.

Arielle's hands land on my chest, and I cover one with my own, squeezing. She sighs, content, as I trail a line of kisses down the column of her neck.

Her dress is a dark blue, the generous neckline showing off her generous tits, and I can't resist the urge to cup them both. I bury my face in her cleavage like I've wanted to all night.

"So you're a boobs guy," Arielle says, breathless, as she runs her hands through my hair.

I shake my head, unbuttoning the tiny buttons making up the bodice of the dress.

"You're not?" She takes my hand away from her sternum, moving to her thick backside, and I curl my fingertips into her flesh. "Are you an ass guy?"

With a wolfish grin, I tell her, "I'm an *Arielle Weiss* kind of guy."

She sighs, her eyes fluttering shut. "Fuck," she whispers.

"Too much?" I pull back.

Quickly, she shakes her head.

"You'll tell me?"

Her head shake turns into a nod, and she bobs her head to the side a few times.

"Healthy communication is—"

Arielle puts her finger against my lips. "Shut up and fuck me."

As my lady commands.

I focus on the rest of the buttons on the front of her dress, pulling the fabric away. She's wearing a silver bra that barely contains her. Her chest rises and falls with her breaths. Once I get her free of her dress, I wrap my arm around her thick waist and tug her down against me.

She throws her leg over my hips, opening her up to me. My hand trails down her flank, memorizing the satin smooth feeling of her skin. She squirms closer, until she's pressed flush against me, my hardness meeting her softness.

Her fingers trail down the column of buttons at the center of my shirt, then she begins to unhook each of them in order. She pushes my shirt off my shoulders, and I move back enough to get free of the fabric and remove my undershirt.

"Hey, Ash," she says, biting her lip.

"Yeah?"

"Take off your fucking pants."

I pull back a bit. "I was planning on—"

"There's time for that later. We'll explore, we'll learn what we like, what works for us. But right now, I need you inside of me."

My cock throbs. I'd like that, too. I'd like nothing more.

"We don't need to rush," I start.

Arielle pulls away. "Do you not want to fuck me?" She tilts her head. "You wouldn't the other night, either. What's going on?"

I sit up on the bed, scratching a hand through my short beard. "Nothing's wrong."

"I didn't say anything was," she says slowly.

"I just—" I blow out a breath. This is embarrassing. I love her, I want to spend the rest of my life with her, and I know—*I know*—we need to have this conversation. We can't start our relationship off without it.

But that doesn't make it easy.

It's not fair to her to keep this a secret. It's not something that I've gone into this intending to hide. It wasn't until we were fooling around the other night that I realized what I wanted—what I *needed*.

"You know I'm bisexual," I tell her.

She nods, her face inscrutable. "That's not news."

"I don't... it's been a long time since I've gone out with a woman," I admit. "The last serious relationship I was in, well..."

"Elliott," she finishes.

I nod. "And well, there are certain parts..."

"Elliott has a penis, I'm guessing."

I quirk a small smile at the clinical phrasing, but the weight of our heavy conversation makes it short-lived.

"And it's not that I haven't been with women since, it's more..."

"You prefer to sleep with men?" She asks.

"I'm attracted to women." I look away. "It's not a preference, it's... anatomy."

"You want something inside of you," she says slowly, her eyes moving rapidly around the room as she processes.

I scrub my hand over my face. "And I know that can be a deal breaker, I know that—"

"Asher, shut up," she snaps.

Flinching, I fall silent.

Her mouth moves as she sounds out words.

"Arielle..." My heart hammers a thousand beats a minute, making me dizzy.

She tilts her head. "Do you need it all the time, or just sometimes?"

"I don't know," I whisper.

"Okay," she says. "Okay."

I swallow. "So... that's it?"

We're over?

This is the end of us—I should have known. She's entitled to have boundaries.

Arielle's eyes snap back to mine. "Do you prefer a plug? Or do you want me to peg you?"

# Arielle

---

A sher stares at me. "You..."

"What?"

He chews his cheek.

"Ash, tell me." I reach for his hand. "Whatever it is, we can get over this hurdle—together."

"You'd be interested? In..."

"Plugs, or pegging?" I blink. "Uh, yes. Very much yes."

"But..."

I squeeze his hand. "Ash, it's me. It's just me."

He lets out a shaky breath. "I just... there's this expectation, you know?"

"Fuck expectations," I tell him sharply.

He shrugs, looking away. "I don't... I know how to do this when I'm with a guy, or someone who presents as male," he says. "When I'm with a woman, I feel like I need to... I don't know." He sighs, scrubs a hand over his face. "It's silly. Like, I recognize that I'm being ridiculous."

"You're not being ridiculous," I tell him.

"I'm supposed to be—I'm supposed to be strong. And know what I want, and go after it, and—"

"It's okay to be strong, and it's okay to let your guard down," I tell him softly. "It's okay to take a while to figure out what you want. And it's okay if you don't pursue it, and you let it come to you, instead."

His dark brown eyes flick to mine, tortured. The pain on his face makes my heart ache.

"I have a question for you," I start.

Guarded, he nods.

"If I told you I wanted to wear a plug, what would you say?"

Asher blinks. He swallows. "You—"

"If I told you I exclusively wanted to try anal, or I didn't want any penetration, or I wanted—whatever it is, if I said that's what I needed to get off, what would you say?" He opens his mouth. "I'm not talking anything illegal, it's all consensual. If I said I needed, x, y, or z, what would you do?"

"I'd move heaven and hell to get it for you," he says, his eyes locked on mine. "Do you—is that what you—"

I shake my head. "Then why can't you believe that I'd do the exact same for you?" I cup his cheek. "Wanting to wear a plug or to be pegged is not anything to be ashamed of. In fact, it's freaking hot."

He winces, turning away. "You're not, like... turned off?"

"At the thought of fucking you?" I laugh. "No, babe. The opposite."

"But..."

"I have an idea," I tell him. "I know it's the last night of Chanukah, and we probably aren't at the exchanging gifts stage yet, but I think we should go shopping for a present tomorrow."

Asher looks at me, confused.

"You mentioned you have toys the other day."

Slowly, he nods.

"A hard limit for me is that I don't want to use anything you've used with a previous partner."

His eyes go wide. "Okay."

"How about we get you a few new toys? Something we can use together?"

"You'd do that?" He whispers. "For me?"

Nodding, I brush my thumb over his lips. "I'd do anything for you."

"Ari..."

"Now, is it just being penetrated, or do you prefer being more submissive in general?" I run my hand through my hair, detangling a knotted curl as my brain moves faster than I can keep up with. "I can work with it either way, I just need to know."

He blinks a few times. "You—you—"

"What?"

"You're okay with this?" He gestures down to his body. "With me being..."

I shrug. "I don't see a reason why I wouldn't like it. I reserve the right to not enjoy it, but I think we're adult enough that we can have a conversation if it's not working."

He looks like he doesn't believe me.

"Asher, you're allowed to have insecurities. You're allowed to sec-ond-guess yourself. You don't always have to be the confident guy who has everything figured out. It's okay to want to experiment."

"I just... I feel like I should know this by now."

"It's okay that you don't." I squeeze his hand. "We're all figuring things out, in one way or another."

"But—"

I cover his mouth with my hand. "It's my turn to talk. It's your turn to listen."

Eyes widening, he nods.

"We're going to have sex," I tell him. "We're going to have a lot of sex. We'll both explore and find what we like. And if we're not compatible, well, then we'll talk about it later. But this? You opening up to me, you sharing this piece of yourself? That's what makes me confident we can get through this."

Slowly, he nods again.

"Now. Go get your favorite toy, and show me how you like to be stretched."

Asher stares at me. "You—you're willing to?"

"Uh, yeah." I blink back at him. "Where have you been the last five minutes?"

"I mean..."

"We're going to try this. I know what I need in order to come. If you're up for it, I can ride your face for a bit, or I can grind on top of you, but I'll get mine—I'm not worried about that. After the other night, I know you can get me there. So now it's your turn. Let's get you feeling good."

Leaning forward, he crushes his lips to mine. "You're amazing," he says, before he kisses me again.

While he's rummaging in his bedside cabinet, I divest myself of my bra and my panties, leaving me naked in the bed. He returns with a small, black plug, a bottle of lube, and a condom.

"I still want to fuck you," he says, "I just need the internal stimulation, too."

"Totally get that."

"You do?"

I shrug. "You like something rubbing up against your prostate. It's the same for me, only in reverse—I need the clitoral stimulation alongside the internal."

Some of the tension fades from his face. "Arielle..."

"Yeah?"

Asher bear-hugs me, wrapping my body around his solid frame. He's hard against my belly, but he doesn't make any move to grind into me or use me for his own pleasure. He's treating me like an equal, not like a toy.

Instead—he kisses my temple, then tightens his arms around me, applying the firm, steady pressure that I need in an embrace.

"How did I get so lucky?" he whispers.

I scratch through the short beard lining his cheeks. "If anything, I think I'm the lucky one."

"You're just so... understanding."

"I think I just understand you," I tell him lightly. "And you understand me."

He kisses me, soft and sweet, as his hand trails down my back. He cups my ass for a moment before he lays me on my back and kisses his way down my body.

"You don't have to," I start.

From between my thighs, Asher looks up at me. "I don't think you understand how much I enjoy this," he says. He spreads my legs further. "I wasn't kidding earlier," he adds. "*This* is my dessert."

He doesn't tease: he dives right in, licking and sucking at me, as his finger traces the slick seam of my entrance. I'm not quite ready for fingers yet. He warms me up, getting me ready for him, until I lose my control of my brain and collapse, helpless to his ministrations. My fingers slide into his hair, and I angle him a bit to the left. When I sigh, he increases his pressure on my clit.

The first press of his finger sends a heady wave of pleasure through me. I tense, and then all of a sudden, my body relaxes. It's at that point that he slips his finger fully inside of me, curling up against my front wall.

I know what he likes now, but he also knows what I like. He gives me firm, unrelenting pressure, much like what I need in an embrace. As Asher adds a second finger, he twists his wrist, and—*ooh*, there, right there. The pressure feels almost insurmountable, it's too much, I can't, there's no escaping this, it's—

With my hands fisting his curls, I come with a cry, the explosion of pleasure so powerful it makes my eyes water.

Asher helps me wind down, his touch lighter now. Chest heaving, I try to work breath back into my lungs, and I tug on his shoulder.

He takes his time, kissing up my body, and I pull him close. I meet his mouth with an eager kiss. He tastes like me, musky and rich.

"How you feeling?" He murmurs against my lips.

I sigh, and he chuckles.

"That good?"

With a laugh, I wrap my arms around his neck and hug on him. "Your ego doesn't need any stroking." My hand travels down his back, then over his hip, to wrap my fingers around his length. "Other parts, however..."

He hitches a gasp when I squeeze him firmly, giving a tentative stroke, then another. The head of his cock is pressed up against my belly, and I shift. Immediately, he moves off of me, and silently we work out a way that we can both be on our sides as I stroke him.

"Do you want me to touch you while you stretch yourself? Or do you want me to stop?"

"Don't stop," he says, his barrel chest heaving as he tries to breathe. "Never stop."

Wiggling backwards, I give him some space.

"Show me."

Asher looks over at me. "Really?"

"Yeah. This time, you're going to get yourself ready," I tell him. "Next time... it'll be me."

His cock jerks in my grasp, and his audible gasp sends lightning through my veins.

"It's absolutely ridiculous that women having something up their ass is supposedly hot, but a man having their prostate played with isn't treated the same. They're equally sexy," I tell him. "I haven't had a lot of experience with it in the past, but I want that to change. Immediately."

He scoots back, reaching for the toy. He brings it around between us. I finger the plug. It's tapered at one end, a solid handle at the other. Asher gulps.

I hand him the lube. "Show me," I repeat.

He slicks his fingers, then rolls to his back, spreading his legs. I move down the bed so I can watch.

He doesn't immediately go for his hole—he starts with his cock, slicking it, stroking it a few times, then cupping his balls and rubbing. His middle finger rubs against his perineum, and then...

Asher's fingers rub around his hole, getting himself ready, rubbing the lube around his rim, as his other hand strokes his cock slowly.

With great patience, he slowly pushes one finger inside himself, only up to the first knuckle. He works it in and out, slowly, slowly, until he's able to fit more inside.

Fire stokes through me at the sight of his finger disappearing inside his slick hole.

Leaning forward, I cover his hand on his cock with mine, increasing the pressure, and then sucking the head into my mouth. He tastes rich and salty, and I absolutely love his natural flavor, even with the lube coating his skin.

Asher grunts, and I feel his wrist moving against my neck.

"You said..." He exhales sharply. "You said you wanted to watch."

I look up at him, letting his cock pop out of my mouth, squeezing the base around his fist. "Do you want me to stop?"

"Fuck."

I kiss the seam of his hip socket, the crease where his pelvis meets his thigh, then work my way down. My hand still on his cock, I rest my cheek on his upper thigh, watching as he works a second finger inside his hole.

"Ash..."

He grunts, his eyes searching mine. Sweat beads at his hairline.

"This is seriously hot," I tell him. "I could watch this forever."

A third finger joins the two. He starts with the tip, stretching around the rim of his hole, before he slips it in to the first knuckle. The original two fingers continue thrusting inside of him, the tendons in his wrist flexing as he touches his inner walls, and slowly he works the third finger in, too. He twists his wrist and—

Asher groans, his cock leaking pre-cum.

"Find it?" I ask.

Breathless, he nods. "Feels so good."

"I want to see the toy."

With a harsh breath, he removes his fingers. His slick hole is stretched open, twitching around the emptiness.

He picks up the toy, slicking it with more lube, then pressing the tapered end against his ass.

He doesn't immediately go for the bullseye, though—he starts slowly, rubbing the tip of the toy around his hole, and it reminds me of how he warmed me up before working his fingers inside of me. He's thorough and careful—in all respects.

Shifting his angle, he pushes the tip of the toy inside. He lets out a short breath, then slowly inserts more and more of the slick silicone plug inside.

His pelvis lifts as he stretches around the toy, until the plug is resting fully inside of him, his hole stretched around the toy.

I stroke his cock. "How you feeling?"

"Full," he breathes.

"Good?"

"So good," he says, nodding quickly. "C'mere."

Crawling back up the bed, I settle next to him, and Asher meets me in a hungry kiss. He rolls onto his side, pulling my leg over his hip, bringing our bodies flush together.

He touches me—all of me. His hands roam over my shoulders, stroke down my back, cup my ass and knead my cheeks before he pulls me even closer. The head of his dick slips between my legs, and I sigh as he hits the perfect angle on my clit to send waves of pleasure radiating through me.

His slick cock rubs against me as he moves his hand to my breast, pinching and rubbing the tight bud of my nipple. It's a full-body attack of pleasure as he learns what makes me feel good, what makes me sigh and what makes me moan.

With his cock between my legs, rubbing against my clit, I ride him as I seek the friction he provides, building pleasure within me.

"Ash," I tell him, demanding.

"Hm?"

"I need you to fuck me."

He smiles. "It would be my pleasure."

My hand moves down to squeeze the base of his dick. "No, actually, I think it will be mine."

"Ours." He kisses the tip of my nose, then twists, searching for the condom behind him. When he finds the foil square, he rips it open. We have to separate in order for him to roll the latex down his length. He adds some lube, stroking it over his cock, then uses the excess as he presses two fingers inside of me. There's no such thing as too much lube.

My eyes fall closed at the unexpected pressure inside of me. It's hard to breathe, in that way where I feel like he's crawled inside my soul and caught hold of my heart and I won't ever be able to survive without him doing this all the fucking time.

Wrapping his arms around me, he returns to that tight, firm embrace, rolling me onto my back and settling above me. Immediately, my legs spread, wrapping loosely around his waist.

Asher guides the head of his cock to my entrance. His eyes search mine.

"I need you," I whisper.

Slowly, he pushes inside of me, hovering halfway. He waits for me to adjust before he grips my hip and thrusts inside.

My head thrown back, I gasp. He rocks forward, until he's buried balls deep inside of me. His heart pounds against mine, a mismatched symphony. I swear my heartbeat tries to sync itself to his.

He squeezes my hip. "Are you feeling okay?"

"Fucking fuck me," I tell him.

Ash grins, kissing me lightly before he pulls back, then thrusts home. My hands clutch ineffectually at his shoulders, trying to hold on as he sets a steady rhythm, varying the pace and searching for new angles until I let out a low groan.

And then he renews his focus. Between the heavy pressure of his body on mine, and the heady pressure of his pelvis grinding against my clit, his thick length inside of me...

I lift my knees higher, and he pushes one leg up, changing the angle. I groan as the pleasure overtakes me, rendering me helpless against the waves of ecstasy.

Once I can breathe again, my arms move low around his waist, hugging him with a lighter touch. I sink my fingers into his ass cheek, and he grunts.

A wicked idea comes to me, and I move my hand between his cheeks. Finding the plug, I press on it with the palm of my hand, putting more pressure on the toy lodged in his ass.

Asher shouts, his entire body tensing. He buries his face in my neck as he comes, breathing heavily.

After a few moments, he pulls out of me, but he doesn't go anywhere. He rests his body weight on top of me, giving me the pressure that he knows I need in an embrace. His softening dick is pressed between my legs. It's a funny kind of sensation. My skin feels oversensitive, but it's a good feeling, like I'm still buzzing from the high.

"How're you doing?" he murmurs, lifting up to make eye contact.

"Good." That's all I can manage right now.

Emotions are cycling through me at a pace so rapid, I'm almost breathless, and my brain is spinning as it tries to process.

He rolls off of me. "Good?"

I nod. "I just..." I'm at a loss for words.

Ash smiles, then kisses me gently. "Good," he says firmly.

The bed dips as he moves away. In the attached bathroom, he deals with the condom and cleans up, and I roll over to watch as he braces an arm on the counter and pulls out the plug. It's seriously hot.

A few minutes later, he returns with a warm, wet flannel, and he cleans me up with slow, loving caresses between my legs.

"Come here," I tell him. He quirks a smile at me, returning the flannel to the bathroom before he crawls back into the bed.

I roll into his arms, resting my head on his shoulder as he wraps his body around me.

I never want this to end.

# Epilogue: Asher

-------------------------------------------------

## Chicago, winter break

We walk into the bar hand-in-hand, and the place goes silent.

I wasn't expecting to be in Chicago so soon after my last trip, but when Arielle mentioned she had a week off at the end of the year coinciding with my school's winter holidays, and she had already planned to visit her family... well, I couldn't let her go face all of our family and friends alone, could I?

"What the fuck," Estee says loudly.

Arielle's hand tightens on mine, and I bring our entwined hands up to my lips, kissing her knuckles in an overt display of affection.

"No fucking way," Noah shouts.

"You guys are seriously together?" Molly asks.

Without hesitation, I say loudly enough for the people in the back of the bar to hear. "Yes, we're together."

Molly shrieks, rushing towards us. She skitters to a stop right in front of us, then throws her arms around me. She pauses, and when Arielle nods, she envelops her in a tight embrace, too.

"I'm so happy for you two!" Molly's typically loud voice is deafening in my ear.

"Thanks, Molls," I say, squeezing her upper arm.

We shared a picture in the group chat of us ice skating at Boston Common with Yoni, Elliott, Sadie, and Rachel with the comment "together at last," but no other context. One of the things I want out of this weekend trip is to take some photos of us together. All the pictures I have of us from growing up are big group shots—I don't think any exist of just the two of us.

Estee shakes herself out of her stupor, making her way over to us. "It's about time!" She elbows me roughly in the ribs. "You've been pining over her for months."

With a sly smile, I tug on one of Estee's curls like I have all our lives. "It was a while, yes," I admit.

Arielle grins up at me. We sat down last weekend and discussed the reason she fled from the wedding, and the insecurity caused by my texting with Estee. I explained that my relationship with Estee is similar to an annoying little sister or cousin, part of my family who has had a tremendous impact on me, but whose opinion has no bearing on my romantic life. And, I added, the only reason I'd started texting Estee after running into Arielle was because I was so desperate for any insight into Arielle's thoughts.

We've both agreed to work on the communication, for the two of us to talk *to* each other instead of *at* each other, and to clearly express when we need time or space to work something out. We have different communication styles, but that doesn't mean we're incompatible; it just means we might have to work at this a bit harder than other couples, and that's okay.

I sling my arm over her shoulders, pulling her into my side. Arielle looks up at me, nerves all over her face. When I drop a kiss on her temple, she relaxes, leaning into me and burying her face in my shoulder.

Noah nods at me from across the room. He jerks his head towards the bar and I nod. With a grin, he disappears into the crowd.

He pops up a few minutes later with two bottles of beer in one hand, and a glass of moscato in the other.

"Congrats, my dudes," he says, handing Arielle the glass of wine. "I'm happy for you."

"Thanks, man." I take the beer he offers me and knock my bottle against his. "L'Chaim."

"You two are so cute," Molly says. "Tell me everything."

"There's not much to tell," Arielle says.

I laugh, and she shakes her head, curling into me.

"Sounds there's a story there," Noah says.

"Well, it really started at Thanksgiving," she says.

"No, at Rosh Hashanah, when we were talking during temple."

She purses her lips. "Or maybe back in Hebrew school?"

"At your Bat Mitzvah." I nudge her.

"High school," Arielle says. She shakes her head. "Well, it's been a long time coming."

"The timing has never been right, and now it is."

We chat with our friends for the better part of an hour. December 24th is one of the busiest nights at Cole's bar, and this year is no exception. The crowd spans through multiple years, from freshly turned 21 to young professionals like our group to people my brother's age, and even older. Everyone who's in town and under forty-five is here.

It's nice being part of the group again. These people were such an important part of my adolescence. I wouldn't be nearly the same without them. They've made me who I am, and they've kept Arielle in my life all these years.

"Hey, I have an idea," I say. I put my empty beer bottle on the nearest table and take her hand in mine. "We should dance."

"Here?" She looks around the crowded bar in confusion.

"Yeah, here."

She sets her wine glass down. "But the music..."

"We can finally cash in on our overdue dance." I kiss her forehead. "You have to promise me something."

Arielle smiles, ducking her head. "What?"

"No more running away."

She laughs, pressing her face into my neck. "I won't."

"Promise?"

"I ran before," she admits. "But you caught me."

Lacing our fingers together, I squeeze her hand. "I did, didn't it?"

"I can't promise I won't get overwhelmed, so if I run... catch me. Chase me. Find me."

"Always," I promise.

# Acknowledgments

----------------------------------------

- Alissa, because lox and everything bagels, tuna fish, and pickles and olives pretty much define us

- Beth, without whom this novella wouldn't exist

- Daniel, because we can pick up right where we left off, no matter the time or distance

- Emily, for asking questions when cultural identity was lost in translation

- Emilie, for endless encouragement and positivity

- Jeffrey, because brisket is brisket is brisket regardless of where you are

- Kyra, for unending friendship, strength, and courage

- Liz Alden, for giving me the courage to take this leap

- Liz Hambleton, because we all need unconditional cheerleading

- Roxanne and family, for welcoming me into your temple community

- Tali, because Mr. Brightside, Zac Efron, and Neville Longbottom will always define our friendship

- My WHIP family and RAW friends, who always have my back

- My SoCalRW family, because I have found my tribe

- Far West USY – we never give up, we always try. From Albuquerque to Waikiki, Far West is the region for me.

# About the Author

------------------------------------------------

Allie Lasky loves writing happy endings... both the PG-13 version and the more risqué variety. In her limited free time, she enjoys spending time with her family and the gremlins, the world's cutest kids. Allie is a San Diego, California native and is allergic to rain, snow, cold weather, and mosquitos.

Join Allie's Facebook group at: www.facebook.com/alliesathletic-supporters/

Follow Allie on Instagram at: www.instagram.com/allielasky/

Sign up for Allie's newsletter at: www.allielasky.com and check out upcoming projects at www.allielasky.com/books/

# Also By Allie

------------------------------------------------

Read THE GAME PLAN to meet sweet cinnamon roll football player Miles and the feisty sorority girl who stole his heart.

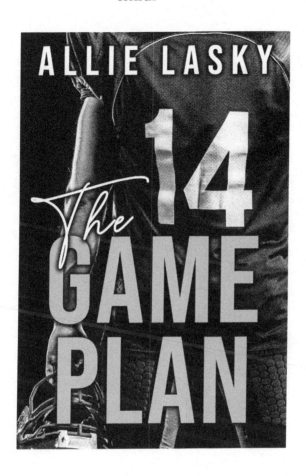

Made in the USA
Monee, IL
20 January 2024

51528644R00074